I0655517

Witness in the Dust

Witness *in the* Dust

Lorrie C. Reed

RESOURCE *Publications* · Eugene, Oregon

WITNESS IN THE DUST

Copyright © 2025 Lorrie C. Reed. All rights reserved. Except for brief quotations in critical publications or reviews, no part of this book may be reproduced in any manner without prior written permission from the publisher. Write: Permissions, Wipf and Stock Publishers, 199 W. 8th Ave., Suite 3, Eugene, OR 97401.

Resource Publications
An Imprint of Wipf and Stock Publishers
199 W. 8th Ave., Suite 3
Eugene, OR 97401

www.wipfandstock.com

PAPERBACK ISBN: 979-8-3852-6449-0
HARDCOVER ISBN: 979-8-3852-6450-6
EBOOK ISBN: 979-8-3852-6451-3

VERSION NUMBER 11/07/25

Contents

CONTENTS

Part IV: Home Away from Home

Abbreviations

CBP	Customs and Border Protection
CDC	Centers for Disease Control
DACA	Deferred Action for Childhood Arrivals
DHS	Department of Human Services
EMT	Emergency Medical Technician
ER	Emergency Room
F-1	Nonimmigrant visa for international students
Form N-400	Naturalization Application Form
GED	General Educational Development
GSW	Gunshot wound
ICE	Immigration and Customs Enforcement
ICU	Intensive Care Unit
ID	Identification
MLK	Martin Luther King
NGO	Non-governmental Organization
SEVIS	Student and Exchange Visitor Information System
SUV	Sport Utility Vehicle
TPS	Temporary Protective Status
UN	United Nations
WHO	World Health Organization

Psalm 24:1-2 (KJV)

The earth is the Lord's, and the fulness thereof; the world, and they that dwell therein. For he hath founded it upon the seas, and established it upon the floods.

Psalm 103:14

For he knows our frame; he remembers that we are dust.

Prologue: Gonaives, Haiti

T he scent of burning palm fronds clung to Pastor Claude's hands as he stood before the plain wooden altar, its purple Lenten drape faded by the dust of last season. Outside the open windows of the Methodist chapel, the sounds of Gonaives seeped in. A donkey cart creaking over rubble, the distant shouts of market vendors hawking tiny portions of rice at prices that made women clutch their empty baskets tighter. The city still bore the scars of Hurricane Noel's destruction from months earlier; streaks of dried mud stained the walls where floodwaters had breached the sanctuary.

The congregation shuffled in, women with headscarves made from flour sacks, men whose Sunday shoes had long since worn out their soles. A toddler whimpered, his belly distended from the hunger. They knelt on the packed-earth floor, their faces turned toward the altar like sunflowers to a storm-choked sky.

Pastor Claude lifted a dented aluminum bowl, the same kind used in Gonaives' slums to serve communal meals, now filled with ashes mixed with precious drops of olive oil. "From dust you came," he intoned, his voice roughened by years of preaching over diesel generators. His thumb marked the first forehead with a cross, the soot sinking into the wrinkles of an elderly deacon who had buried three grandchildren after the floods. The ashes were gritty with more than palm remnants; some came from banana leaves burned in the churchyard, others from charred debris of homes swept away in the hurricane.

A teenage girl approached, her school uniform hanging loose after months of skipped meals. As the pastor pressed his thumb to her forehead, she winced, not from pain, but at the memory of UN troops scattering protesters near the market with rubber bullets. "To dust you shall return," Claude murmured. The cross on her skin mirrored the chalked X's on buildings marked for demolition.

The altar, bare except for a communion plate holding cassava wafers and a pitcher of grape juice shipped from Miami, became an island of order. A woman with blistered fingertips laid a pouch of coins beside it, her week's wages, destined for the food fund. The unvarnished wood, scarred by termites and candle wax, bore the weight of Haiti itself: Here, Christ's sacrifice was not abstract. The juice might be the only sweet thing some tasted for weeks; the bread, a reminder of stomachs that would remain unfilled despite the fasting season.

When the final hymn began, a Creole translation of "Just As I Am" sung over the arrhythmic clatter of a lone tambourine, the altar cloth fluttered in the hot wind. Dust motes swirled in the shafts of light, catching on the tears of a man whose whispered prayer was lost beneath the sound of his hunger cramps.

As the benediction ended, the congregation rose, their ashen crosses declaring a truth deeper than the riots, deeper than the poverty: Mortality was the one democracy Gonaives still had. They walked back into the bleaching sunlight and past walls plastered with peeling campaign posters for politicians who had promised redemption. The altar stood empty behind them, a table set in the wilderness, holding only the ghosts of prayers and the lingering smell of smoke. The call to "remember you are dust" carried both spiritual weight and stark physical reality in a city where dust from eroding hillsides, crumbling buildings, and unpaved roads was an inescapable daily reality.

PART I

Gonaives, Haiti—August 2008

1

A Day in the Life

July 2008

T he years between 2008 and 2010 were a relentless trial for Haiti, a nation already weathered by hardship. Nature itself seemed to conspire against the island, unleashing catastrophe after catastrophe upon its people, each disaster deepening the wounds left by the last. Haiti, perched on the storm-lashed rim of the Caribbean and straddling the uneasy border between tectonic plates, had long known suffering, but seldom had the earth and sky aligned so cruelly against it.

In 2008, the storms struck one after another, as if fueled by a merciless tide. First Fay, then Gustav, then Hanna, then Ike, each hurricane tore through the country, leaving rivers swollen beyond their banks, hillsides sliding into destruction, and fields submerged under thick layers of mud. Homes collapsed like wet paper; roads disappeared beneath torrents of debris. The earth couldn't hold the rain, and the rain refused to stop. Crops failed, hunger spread, and families fled their villages with only what they could carry on their backs. The land itself seemed to rebel, refusing shelter and sustenance.

This was a time when survival required more than just endurance; it demanded defiance. Against storms and the gradual creep of hunger and despair, the people of Haiti pressed on, step by step, through the wreckage of their world.

###

The first fingers of dawn stretched over the horizon, painting the Caribbean Sea in molten gold as turquoise waves lapped against the shore, their rhythm a lazy beat against the morning quiet. The air buzzed with the scent of salt and the rich fragrance of tropical blossoms, their waxy petals fluttering in the gentle breeze.

Inside the Laurent home, sunlight streamed through open windows, casting warm streaks across the floor. The scent of woodsmoke and frying plantains drifted through the air as Mireille moved between the stove and the table, her bare feet shuffling against the smooth, worn floorboards. Beads of sweat glistened along her brow as she stirred a pot of rice porridge, the rich, nutty aroma rising with each turn of her wooden spoon. Her headscarf, the color of ripe tamarind, had slipped just enough to let a few braids escape, clinging to her neck in the humid air.

David sat in his usual chair by the door, calloused hands resting on his knees, hands that knew the weight of a hoe, the ache of flooded rice fields, the stubborn earth that yielded little but demanded everything. The sun had etched its story into his skin, leaving behind deep valleys around his eyes and mouth. He watched his wife, Mireille, work, the way her shoulders rolled with each motion, the soft clink of her bracelets keeping time with her movements. The thought of her at the market later, bartering with a voice like warm honey, made his chest swell.

Then, with a whirl of energy, Celine, their daughter, burst into the room, her braids swinging against her back like ropes of polished mahogany. The scent of coconut oil trailed behind her, mingling with a trace of lye soap on her sun-warmed skin.

"Mama, can I help?" Her voice was bright as the morning, eager as the roosters crowing outside.

Mireille turned, and the smile that spread across her face was like a lantern flickering to life. "No. I've got this part under control, my love," she said, reaching to tuck a stray braid behind Celine's ear, her fingers brushing against the girl's cheek, warm and familiar.

David rose then, his joints protesting with gentle creaks, to set the table. The clay bowls clicked softly against the wood as he placed them, each one worn smooth from years of use.

"It smells good," he murmured, his voice rough as tree bark. The porridge bubbled, its steam curling into the air, thick and comforting.

Mireille ladled the creamy rice into their bowls, the scent of cinnamon and condensed milk rising in sweet clouds. Then she sat, reaching for their hands. Celine's palm was soft against her mother's work-roughened one, David's grip firm and steady.

"Before we eat," Mireille began, her voice a low, sure current, "let us give thanks."

And in that moment, the room held its breath, the taste of salt on their lips, the hum of the waking world outside, and the warmth of their joined hands, a fragile, perfect thing, suspended in the golden light.

The coastal air in Gonaives carried the salty smell of the sea, mingling with woodsmoke from morning cookfires. Red dust, fine as ground cayenne, coated every surface, crunching underfoot and settling on lips with a gritty dryness. The marketplace came alive as vendors arranged their wares: pyramids of ripe plantains shining with morning dew, burlap sacks bursting with coffee beans that released their earthy aroma when jostled, and baskets of dried codfish whose sharp saltiness cut through the humid air.

Old radios crackled with kompa music, their tinny melodies competing with the bleating of goats tied to splintered fence posts. Women in vibrant headwraps haggled over rice prices, their rapid-fire Creole punctuated by sharp claps when striking a deal. The scent of pikliz, fermented cabbage and scotch bonnet peppers, made eyes water as it wafted from food stalls, where sizzling pork griot popped in shallow pans of bubbling oil.

Near the midway's edge, Mama Adjoa arranged her spiritual goods with gnarled fingers. Her stall smelled of aged leather and frankincense, with beaded packets and carved wooden figures sitting beside practical herbs for fever and childbirth. A gentle breeze carried greetings, with the syllables blending into the rhythmic ebb and flow of waves against the nearby pier.

Children's bare feet slapped against the sunbaked earth as they darted between stalls, sneaking bites of sugarcane that dripped sticky-sweet juice down their wrists. Somewhere, a drum started its relentless beat, calling the city's rhythm into the growing heat.

Celine's bare feet touched the rain-drenched ground as she entered the marketplace, cool mud squelching between her toes, the lingering scent of petrichor still hanging in the air. The scrape of stools being dragged across stone blended with the sleepy hum of vendors as they started their day. She weaved through the crowd, the coarse fabric of her worn dress brushing softly against her calves with each step.

Near the spice stalls, the rich sweetness of cinnamon and nutmeg filled the air. Madame Dupont's gnarled hands trembled as she held a jar of cloves, her arthritic fingers slipping on the glass, now slick with condensation. Celine caught the warm, woody scent as she twisted the lid free with a satisfying pop. The older woman's grip felt papery against her wrist. Her whispered thanks carried the faintest hint of ginger tea.

At the butcher's stall, flies buzzed lazily over strips of meat drying in the sun, their wings humming like tiny engines. Celine adjusted her wide-brimmed hat, the woven fibers scratching her temples as she covered her mouth to block the ferric stench.

A whimper sliced through the noise. Little Rosalie crouched in the dirt, her knee bleeding where the skin had split on sharp stones. Celine knelt, the frayed edge of her handkerchief catching on the girl's scraped flesh. Rosalie's breath hitched, warm and salty with tears, until Celine pressed their foreheads together. "Breathe," she murmured, filling the space between them with the scent of lemongrass and lye soap.

A crash sounded near the booth where Jean-Luc's charcoal sack had torn, sending brittle black fragments skittering across the stones. The sharp, burnt smell of wood filled Celine's nose as she gathered the pieces into her apron, soot staining her palms gray. When she helped him adjust the sack on his narrow shoulders, the rough burlap scraped against his sunburned skin.

A shadow crossed Celine's path. Monsieur Dupont offered her a skewer of grilled pork, the fat sizzling, the crust charred and shimmering. Celine's mouth flooded with saliva as she took a bite, the melted fat coating her tongue with smoky richness. Around her, the market buzzed: the rhythmic slap of sandals on stone, the crack of sugarcane being split, the bright peal of laughter piercing the drone of haggling voices.

Nearby, in the medical tent, the sterile scent of alcohol wipes mingled with the sour odor of sweat. Dr. Patrice Sinclair's cool fingers pressed against the feverish brow of a toddler, whose breathing wheezed like a deflating balloon. The nebulizer hissed to life, its plastic mouthpiece clicking against tiny teeth as medicinal mist filled the cramped space, sharp and chemical, cutting through the damp blanket smell.

By dusk, the clinic table was littered with empty vials that gleamed dull in the fading light. The humanitarian medical team packed their truck, muscles aching, the taste of dust and exhaustion thick on their tongues. As the engine coughed to life, the marketplace carried on, the peppery bite of crushed spices hanging in the air, dominoes clacking against wooden tables, and the rhythmic thud of mortar against pestle keeping time like a heartbeat.

The medical truck drove off, tires kicking up red dust that settled like fine powder over everything it touched. Behind them, Gonaives breathed, hungry, relentless, alive, as the last rays of sunlight faded into the horizon. Tomorrow, the medics would return. And the dance in the marketplace would start again.

Gabriel found Celine by the seashore at sunset, the damp earth still holding the heat of the sun beneath its cooling surface. He lowered himself beside her, his shoulder brushing against hers, their warm skin meeting, the scent of sunbaked cotton lingering on both of them.

Celine kicked off her sandals, wiggling her toes into the gritty sand that still held onto the warmth of the afternoon. Gabriel slumped forward, elbows pressing into his thighs, fingers tapping a restless rhythm against his shins, tap-tap-tap, like rain on a tin roof. The air smelled of moist earth and something heavier, something lingering.

She didn't need to look at him to know where his thoughts had drifted. The sky hung heavy and gray, like weathered stone, pressing down on them. Beyond the horizon, the clouds grew thicker.

Then, rustling fabric. Celine's hand emerged from her pocket holding two pieces of peanut brittle, their edges uneven from where they'd been broken. The sweet aroma of caramelized sugar filled the air before she even offered one to Gabriel, the roasted peanuts embedded in the golden slab catching the fading light.

"I nearly forgot about these," she said.

Gabriel took it, his dry skin and rough calluses brushing against hers. He let out a quiet laugh, a familiar sound like the creak of their old school benches.

"Haven't we had enough sugar for the day?" Gabriel asked.

Celine put her piece in her mouth, the candy breaking with a snap, first the crisp crack of caramel, then the hearty, earthy crunch of peanuts. A rush of salt and sweetness flooded her tongue.

"Nope." She grinned, sticky crumbs catching at the corner of her mouth. "I could always use more sugar."

Gabriel rolled his eyes but continued to suck on the candy, allowing it to dissolve slowly, the bitter taste of burnt sugar lingering on his lips.

For a while, they said nothing. The breeze carried the last whispers of the marketplace, the clatter of folding stalls, the distant call of a mother rounding up her children, and the low hum of a radio playing somewhere in the distance.

Celine tilted her head back, watching the bruised purple of twilight seep into the sky. The sun dipped lower, its fading light catching the dust in the air, turning it to gold.

Somewhere, rain was approaching. But for now, just this: two friends sharing a candy break. The crunch of brittle between teeth. The innocent press of a shoulder against another. The quiet understanding of two people who had known each other's silences as long as they'd known each other's voices.

The scent of kerosene and simmering onions hung in the kitchen air as Celine lingered in the doorway, her bare feet pressing into the warped floorboards, their grooves worn smooth by generations of footsteps. The single bulb overhead buzzed weakly, casting a jaundiced glow that made the shadows in the corners pulse.

Mireille's silhouette sat straight and tall at the kitchen table; her work-worn hands moved with the slow precision of exhaustion. A calloused thumb traced the edge of the envelope, thin, foreign paper that crackled like dried leaves when unfolded. The ink smelled faintly chemical, the blue script bleeding slightly where Chicago's dampness had touched it.

"Come," she said, motioning for Celine to sit at the table next to her.

Mireille opened the letter, catching a faint whiff of distant city smells, diesel, cooking oil, and the scents of Pierre's community center clinging to the fibers. Mireille's lips moved silently over the Creole phrases, each word settling like grit. Celine, too, could sense the bitterness in her mother's exhale when Pierre wrote of men who spoke to him "like I'm simple," and could feel the phantom ache in her own shoulders at the mention of his unrelenting back pain.

Then, the MoneyGram, startling white against the table's scarred wood, caught her eye. Mirielle picked it up. The paper was stiff as a dried corn husk between her fingers. Two hundred dollars. The numbers stared back at them; the ink slightly raised under Mirielle's tentative touch.

A hollow sound echoed through the house as the wind pressed against the shutters. Somewhere beyond the mango tree, a dog's bark pierced the night, sharp and persistent. The kitchen clock's pendulum swung, each tick like a grain of sand falling in an hourglass, marking the gap between here and Chicago, between sacrifice and survival.

Mireille tucked the MoneyGram into the fold of her bra, where it would soak up her sweat and the numbers might smudge but never disappear. The wind gusted again, carrying the salty scent of the distant sea and the damp promise of rain on the way.

2

Prelude to a Storm

AUGUST 2008

The morning air clung to the skin like a damp shirt, heavy with the salty smell of fish drying on bamboo racks. Beneath all of that, the rich scent of rain-soaked earth rose in waves with the August breeze. Soon, it would be time for school to start. Preparations were in progress.

The international charitable organizations arrived, as they do every year, to provide humanitarian and medical aid to Haitian children preparing for the new school year. The trucks rolled in before dawn, their engines rumbling as they unloaded boxes filled with pencils, bandages, and bottles of pink amoxicillin syrup for the annual back-to-school visit. They moved with the quick efficiency of people who believe in solutions, their knuckles brushing against the rough edges of packing tape, and their starched collar fabrics whispering against sweat-damp necks. Sister Therese, a no-nonsense perfectionist, stood guard beside Pastor Claude, her voice scraping like a match strike.

"Move the pencils and crayons to the back table," she said, while her fingers, knotted with arthritis, fingered the cross around her neck like a worry stone.

Pastor Claude balanced a stack of notebooks as he adjusted his grip, their new pages giving off a light chemical smell of inexpensive paper.

Their debate about the distribution table unfolded in hissed Creole and fractured English, punctuated by the thud of boxes hitting dirt.

"There must be order. No mobs," Pastor Claude insisted, rubbing his temples as if pushing back a tide. His breath carried the harsh scent of overly strong coffee; it was the kind brewed thick enough to stand a spoon in.

Sister Therese huffed as she arranged the school supplies on the designated table.

By midmorning, the mango tree's dappled shade cradled their folding tables, its branches sagging with unripe fruit that dripped sticky sap onto the ground. The line of mothers swayed like a human river, sweat making blouses stick to their backs, bare feet shuffling through dust, and the sour-milk smell of a baby's spit-up cutting through the scent of fear. Having waited in line for too long, the mothers started to push toward the school supply tables. A wail tore through the air. A bottle shattered. A wave of bodies crashed against the fragile barricade of folding chairs, and a stampede surged forward. And just like that, the illusion of order broke apart.

At the uniform distribution station, the crowd swelled, a living thing, its voice a cacophony of Creole and desperation. A man's shout sliced through the noise.

"They won't take my son without a uniform!" His hands clawed at the air. Pastor Claude stayed steady, but Sister Therese quickly stepped in to prevent a confrontation.

"No worries," she said. "We can alter last year's uniform." She saw the man's shoulders sag as the fight left him.

Celine accompanied Dr. Sinclair, who had begun her rounds at the makeshift outdoor clinic. The scent of fever rose from a young girl's skin, sour with sweat. After waiting for Dr. Sinclair's nod of approval, Celine grabbed a clean rag, its fibers rough in her palms. She soaked the cloth with purified water, droplets splattering onto the dusty ground. The girl whined when the damp fabric touched her forehead, her cracked lips parting in a silent gasp.

"Hold on," Celine murmured in Creole, her voice honey-thick as her thumbs traced circles on the girl's clammy temples. The girl's mother sat silently, her calloused hands kneading the hem of her dress into a wrinkled knot. "She'll be okay," Celine whispered to the mother.

A nurse stepped beside them, pressing a water bottle into the mother's trembling hand. Her words were gentle, meant to comfort, but Celine noticed the way the mother's eyes darted, looking beyond the doctor, past the nurse, searching for something steady. The mother fixed her gaze on Celine, instantly calming her suspicions as her fingers clutched the water bottle like a lifeline.

Overhead, the sky darkened as the mango leaves trembled like frightened children. The wind intensified, carrying the smell of the approaching storm. Thunder rumbled in the distance, a deep growl from the earth's throat.

The first warning didn't come through clouds or wind, but through the air itself, thick and salty. The humidity pressed down until every breath felt like swallowing the ocean. Even the palm trees seemed to be hunching under pressure, their fronds whispering secrets in a language only the old fishermen understood.

Gabriel stood on the shoreline, his bare feet sinking into the sand still warm from the afternoon sun. The Caribbean Sea stretched out before him, its surface like hammered silver under the fading light. But beneath that shimmering surface, he could sense it, the slow, restless churn of deep water, with currents coiling like serpents ready to strike. The smell of brine was heavy, mixed with something darker, alive with storm energy.

Standing beside him, Celine tilted her face up toward the sky, sensing the change before she saw it, the flicker of lightning in the wind, the way her braids lifted slightly, pulled by invisible fingers. She noticed the women gathering near the tideline, murmuring prayers, their voices swallowed by the growl of waves hitting the rocks. Further down the beach, children still played, their laughter sharp as gulls' cries against the mounting tension. Their bare feet kicked up clouds of sand that stung like pinpricks when the wind blew them back.

The first heavy raindrops fell with loud splats, darkening the ground like blood on cloth. Then the wind stirred, not with a gust, but with a groan deep in the sky's belly. It rattled the shutters on the fishing huts and sent coconut husks tumbling like dice across the sand. The rain intensified, stinging the skin and soaking clothes until they clung like a second skin.

Although the sea roared its challenge, the villagers responded with something even fiercer: memory, spirit, and the unwavering belief that storms pass, but the soul of Gonaives never breaks. Their bodies formed a living barrier against the storm, their joined hands a chain no flood could wash away. The taste of salt on their lips might have come from the sea, tears, or stubborn hope. As the wind howled through the streets, the people felt reassured that they would survive. Again.

Tropical Storm Fay: August 15-19, 2008

August 15th arrived with the smell of wet earth and fear, Tropical Storm Fay crashing into the coast like a starving animal. The first gust hit Celine directly in the chest as she stacked sandbags. The rain came not in drops but in sheets, ice-cold needles stabbing her arms, soaking through her clothes. She gasped as the downpour flooded her mouth with the taste of the ocean's fury concentrated into water. Beside her, Gabriel, heaving debris, shouted something, but the wind carried away his words, leaving only the feeling of his fingers gripping Celine's wrist.

Inside, the house groaned under the storm's weight. Candle flames flickered in their jars, casting shaky shadows that made the walls seem alive. The tin roof screeched with each gust, the sound like nails being dragged across metal. Mirielle pressed her forehead to the shutter slats, the wood rough against her skin. Through the cracks, she watched the world unravel, palm trees bent double, their fronds whipping like frayed ropes; the market stalls cracking apart with sounds that echoed like gunshots.

Somewhere amid the chaos, the sea roared a warning, a deep, guttural sound that vibrated in Mirielle's teeth. She thought of the fishing boats, their hulls cracking like eggshells; of the cassava fields drowning in the surge; of the old women's palm-frond crosses, their woven symbols of faith now just debris swirling in the flood.

By midday, the wind grew fiercer. It tore through the village, shredding tarps, uprooting fences, and hurling coconuts like cannonballs. The roads disappeared beneath knee-deep water, with the current tugging at ankles. Children's laughter was drowned out by the storm's howling. The market collapsed, with wood splintering and baskets of rice and beans turning into sludge.

And the sea. It wasn't just water anymore. It was a living thing, a monster. Waves crashed against the shore with enough force to shake the ground, their spray stinging like wasps. The air reeked of crushed vegetation, rotting fish, mud, and gasoline as the storm consumed the village whole.

Three days.

Three days of roofs tearing away like scabs. Of rivers vomiting over their banks, carrying off everything: chickens, Bibles, the corpse of a goat, its stiff legs jutting skyward.

And then, silence. Not peace, never peace, but the absence of wind. The people emerged like ghosts, stepping over the carcass of their homes. They moved slowly, their hands brushing broken wood, their feet sinking into mud that sucked at their heels like quicksand. A child's sandal. A waterlogged photograph. A single surviving mango, its skin bruised but still clinging to the branch.

They had no time to mourn. Because the horizon was already darkening again, the sky warned of Hurricane Gustav, its hot, foul breath pressing down on them like judgment.

But the people stood. Bent, yes. Bruised, always. But unbroken.

Hurricane Gustav: August 27, 2008

Celine knew Gustav was coming before the first palm fronds started to sway. She stood in the doorway, the wind already sharp like a knife, licking salt and sweat from her lips. The sea, still swollen from Fay's tantrum, rose in large, heaving gulps, hurling waves over the breakwater with a sound like boulders cracking open.

"It's worse this time," Gabriel said, his voice raw. Celine didn't answer.

The rain hit sideways, stinging exposed skin and turning dirt roads into rushing brown rivers within minutes. The wind screamed through gaps in the walls, snuffing out candles with icy fingers and stealing the breath from their lungs. Somewhere nearby, a roof tore away, its tin panels clattering like a skeleton dragged across stone.

For three days, Gustav raged.

At the hospital, the tent flap swung open with a wet slap, and Celine slipped inside, her braids heavy with rainwater, her arms holding a plastic-wrapped bundle. She unrolled it with stiff fingers. It contained boiled rags, still steaming, the sharp smell of antiseptic rising from them.

"For cleaning wounds," she said, pressing them into the nurse's hands. The heat of them lingered on her palms.

Dr. Sinclair didn't look up from the child's split forehead as she stitched with the last sterile thread, the needle flashing. A nurse pressed a scrap of paper into her gloved hand.

"Port-au-Prince can't send supplies. Roads are gone," the nurse reported. Dr. Sinclair's jaw tightened, but her hands never wavered.

"Okay," she muttered. "We work with what we have."

At the Methodist shelter, the air crackled with panic, shouts, sobs, and the sharp smell of sweat and fear. A woman wailed, her voice raw, her life overwhelmed by the flood. Sister Therese appeared with a chipped enamel cup, guiding the woman's trembling hands around it. From her sack came a green coconut: one swift machete stroke, a straw wedged into the soft flesh inside.

"Sip," she ordered. "Slowly."

Pastor Claude staggered in later, hauling a half-sack of rice, his shirt plastered to his back. "Got some rice," he panted. "Not enough."

Dr. Sinclair didn't hesitate. "Get it to the school. The kids haven't eaten since yesterday."

Celine was already there, stirring a pot of thin porridge over a flickering fire. She had taken a bit of cinnamon from her mother's stash, just enough to make hungry stomachs believe it was more than just water and grain. When the first child whimpered, she ladled the gruel into a tin cup, blew on it until the steam rose, then pressed it into small hands.

For the rest of the afternoon, she moved through the wreckage like a needle through torn fabric, quick, precise, leaving no trace but the mended tear.

And when the rain finally stopped, it was her voice, steady as a drumbeat, that told the children to look up. The clouds were breaking.

The silence was the first surprise, not just quiet, but a thick, cottony hush that pressed against Celine's eardrums after days of wind's howling. Celine stepped outside, her bare feet sinking into the mud. It oozed between her toes, warm and gritty with broken pottery, shattered glass, and the unseen debris of their lives. The air smelled like soaked earth and something sour underneath, maybe rotting fruit, or the damp breath of flooded cellars.

Sister Therese and a group of boys pushed aside a fallen beam. Dust and the sharp scent of wet concrete filled the air. One of them straightened, victorious, holding up a tin pot, battered but intact, its bottom blackened from years of fires.

"Take this," Sister Therese said, pressing it into the hands of a woman with hollow eyes. The pot clattered slightly, her fingers trembling. "We'll bring food by noon."

Pastor Claude trudged past, arms loaded with a box of donated soap, the sharp, medicinal smell of lye cut through the rot. "The Methodists are sending more supplies next week," he said, breathing hard.

"Next week." Sister Therese rolled the words in her mouth. They tasted like dust, with an aftertaste reminiscent of old rainwater.

Hurricane Hanna: September 1-3, 2008

Hurricane Hanna didn't scream like the others. She exhaled.

The floodwaters first appeared as a shimmering black line where the sky met the land, a distant ripple carrying the scent of impending rain. The air grew thick and heavy, infused with the greenish-yellow pallor of decaying fruit, pressing down on Gonaives until every breath felt like damp rot.

At the Methodist shelter, Pastor Claude waded through waist-deep water that had turned murky with sewage and silt. The protein bars in his hands softened inside their wrappers, their edges turning into sticky paste. An older woman clutched his forearm, her fingers digging into his flesh with surprising strength.

"I need clean water," she rasped, her throat raw from thirst.

The words barely registered above the slick slap-slap of bodies moving through floodwaters, the gurgling protests of empty stomachs, and the high, thin wails of children who had cried themselves hoarse. Claude yelled for purification tablets, knowing the chlorine's chemical bite would only go so far.

The bloated corpse of a goat floated in the water, its fur flattened and its belly swollen with gas. The smell of decay rose with the floodwaters, thick enough to coat the tongue.

"Even the animals couldn't outrun this," Claude murmured.

And then, with the same indifference with which she arrived, Hanna sighed and drifted away. A lone, sharp church bell rang out, defiant, its tone cutting through the smell of wet rot and despair.

Hurricane Ike: September 4-14, 2008

Hurricane Ike started with a heavy, oppressive air that hadn't yet decided to storm, thick with the smell of wet concrete and the ozone smell of nearby lightning. By afternoon, the sky turned a sickly yellow-green like an old bruise, completely swallowing the sun.

Then came the water.

Not the crashing waves of earlier storms but a slow, insidious creep that brushed doorways, then windowsills, then swallowed entire streets with quiet malice. The flood carried its own smells, rotting vegetation, the sharp bite of gasoline from overturned drums, the warm iron scent of blood where debris had torn flesh.

Lightning flashed like a camera's intense strobe, capturing jagged moments in frozen snapshots.

EMTs from the Haiti Health Foundation, their uniforms clinging like second skins, faces streaked with rain and exhaustion, lifted a pregnant woman onto a makeshift stretcher. Her moans mingled with the wet slap of their footsteps through chest-high water.

Catholic Relief workers formed a human chain, their arms burning as they passed water bottles hand to hand to a stranded family. The plastic crinkled, and the labels had long since dissolved into pulp.

The Food for the Poor depot collapsed inward, with burlap rice sacks bursting like overripe fruit, their contents swirling into the rising tide, the starchy smell of dissolving grains mixed with the salt-stench of floodwater.

3

After the Hurricanes

T he air in the Methodist church was heavy, filled with the damp smell of wood and mildew. Bodies pressed shoulder to shoulder on warped pews, their sweat mixing with the scent of palm oil still lingering on Sunday-best dresses now stiff with dried floodwater.

Pastor Claude allowed the silence to stretch until it became painful. Then, the spine of his Bible groaned as he opened it. When he spoke, his voice sounded like charcoal scraping across stone.

"I cried out to God for help."

The psalm fell silent, like a rock sinking into still water. His cracked lips carefully formed each word with weight:

"My hand was stretched out in the night and did not grow weary. . ."

A baby whimpered nearby. Somewhere, a man's calloused fingers fiddled with the frayed hem of his shirt.

Pastor Claude's gaze swept the room, over hollow cheeks, over hands still covered with mud from digging graves.

"You think the Psalmist didn't doubt?" A bitter laugh rattled in his chest. "'Has the Lord forgotten me?' No, the Psalmist screamed just like you screamed when the current ripped your doorframes apart. Just like I screamed," his knuckles whitened on the pulpit, "when I pulled a child's shoe from the sludge and knew the stitchwork from my own wife's hands."

The kerosene lamp sputtered, casting a large shadow on the wall, a flickering giant of grief and fury.

"But listen!" The Bible thumped against the wood. "Hear what comes after the weeping!" His voice swelled, raw and resonant:

"I will remember the deeds of the Lord. . . Your path led through the sea, Your way through the mighty waters, though Your footprints were not seen!"

A current ran through the room, a sharp intake of breath, the creak of a pew as someone leaned forward.

Claude stepped down, his boots scraping damp sawdust from the flood. Lamplight caught the sweat at his temples as he pointed to the shattered window where clouds hovered over flooded fields.

"God doesn't promise calm waters." His words dripped like honey and vinegar. "Doesn't promise your sandals won't fill with grit or your palms won't blister from the oar. Just says you'll pass through."

A whisper of metal. A woman's tambourine trembled, once, a shivering sigh. Then again, louder, with the jingles biting through the thick air.

Claude's voice rose like a wave: "The God who split the sea hears your *why* and thunders back, *walk!*"

The church erupted. Tambourines shook like thunder. A teenager's boots thudded on the floorboards.

"We go through!" Claude roared over the cacophony, his teeth flashing white in the gloom. "Not around. Not over. Through."

The tambourines paused just long enough to catch his last words, softer now, like a soothing balm on the raw night.

"And on the other side?" His calloused hand opened toward the congregation. "We will replant what the waters believed they stole."

###

After the storms, the church was left broken, its walls had yielded to the wind, and some of its wooden pews were shattered like kindling. The hurricane had been indiscriminate in its destruction.

Pastor Claude's hands rested on the shattered wood of what used to be the communion table. He exhaled slowly, as if measuring grief by his breath. Behind him, Celine and Mireille sifted through the debris, lifting pieces of stained glass like scattered jewels. The altar, once the centerpiece of every prayer, lay in fragments beneath a fallen beam.

Celine ran her fingers along the remains of the altar cloth, its embroidery frayed and dirty. "I wonder where God is now," she stated without emotion.

Pastor Claude straightened himself. "Maybe we've been wrong about where altars must be." He turned his palm upward, an empty gesture, but filled with significance. "David wrote: 'The sacrifices of God are a broken spirit.' If your heart is shattered, and yet you still call His name, isn't that the truest altar?"

Mireille let out a sharp, unsteady laugh. "Easy for a pastor to say. Tell that to the people who lit candles here, who knelt on these tiles. Will prayers in the dirt feel just as sacred?"

"They did for Abraham." Claude's voice was quiet. "He built altars out of wilderness stones, not because God needed them, but because Abraham needed them. Maybe we've been given the same lesson."

Celine wiped her hands on her skirt, leaving streaks of dust. "So, we don't rebuild the destroyed altars?"

Pastor Claude hesitated. "We rebuild people first." His gaze wandered beyond the ruined church to the battered houses, uprooted trees, and makeshift shelters where families huddled. "The altars will now occupy the sacred places in our hearts. Our candles will light up the darkness with the inner lights we carry. And if what we carry inside is holy, then every meal we share with the hungry is communion. Every time we lift someone's grief, that's the sacrifice."

Mireille studied him intently. Then she reached into her pocket and placed a single, unlit candle on the broken altar slab. "Fine. But I'm keeping the matches."

The wind shifted, lighter now, almost gentle. As if something unseen had stepped into the ruins, not to mourn what was lost, but to hallow what remained.

Inside the skeletal remains of the church, Pastor Claude broke protein bars into halves and then quarters. The smell of peanut butter and artificial vanilla stuck to his fingers. A man with lips split from thirst took his portion, looked at it, then threw it to the ground.

"Biscuits won't bring back my son!"

The wrapper landed with a quiet plop, the Red Cross logo bleeding into the water like a dying sigh.

A truck rumbled through Celine's neighborhood. She didn't turn. She knew the routine by heart now, the diesel roar, the hollow thump of empty rice sacks hitting the ground, and the way foreign volunteers would press a hand to her shoulder and murmur "God bless" in French accents thicker than the mud caked under her nails.

She flexed her fingers. The salt from evaporated sweat itched on her palms. Somewhere, a motorcycle sputtered to life again, time to keep moving.

The sound of hammers echoed through the marketplace, broken up by the occasional shout of a World Vision coordinator guiding a group of local builders. Gabriel wiped sweat from his brow with the back of his wrist, his shirt sticking to his back. When he caught Celine's eye across the scaffolding, his smile was warm and slow, like sunlight breaking through storm clouds.

A boy kicked a deflated soccer ball past them, a donation from a Florida church group, with the stitching already coming apart. Celine intercepted it, her bare foot kicking up a puff of dust. Gabriel, now standing beside her, caught her elbow as she stumbled, his grip warm and firm.

"Careful," he murmured, thumb tracing the scar on her forearm, left by a collapsing roof during Hanna.

She leaned into his touch. "They're saying the medical convoy from Doctors Without Borders is coming tomorrow."

Gabriel snorted. "They said that last week."

He threw his head back and laughed, a sound so rare these days that a Red Cross nurse paused mid-stride to smile. Their joy felt dangerous, like lighting a candle in a hurricane. But it was theirs.

Dr. Sinclair's boots sank into the mud behind the hospital with a wet, sucking sound. Her throat burned not only from exhaustion but also from knowing that the WHO shipment of oral rehydration salts was still somewhere in Port-au-Prince. A child whimpered nearby, his skin hot under her fingers, his breath sour with dehydration. She replayed the scene running through her mind.

Near the collapsed bridge, the UN trucks sat like stranded whales, their white paint streaked with mud. A Haitian Red Cross worker slapped the side of a motorcycle taxi, her voice cracking as she begged the driver to hurry. The cooler strapped to the bike was already sweating; the ice packs inside were sloshing as they melted. "Go, go, before the vaccines spoil!" The worker said.

Somewhere, the last drops of rain tapped from a bent gutter into a puddle, its rhythm uneven, like a fading heartbeat. Inside the Laurent home, Mirielle scanned the rooms one last time before the guests arrived. The kerosene lamp near the kitchen sputtered when Mirielle touched the match to its wick. The light cast shadows that flicked at the damp walls, their mildew-sweet scent mixing with the sharp sting of burning fuel.

After everyone had finished the last of the humble meal and the table had been cleared, everyone gathered for a serious discussion. Dr. Sinclair's fingers rasped against the wrinkled map as she spread it across the kitchen table, its edges curling like dried leaves. The air was thick with the bitter aroma of over-brewed coffee. Celine cradled her chipped mug, the heat seeping into her palms as she inhaled its dark, earthy steam.

"Port-au-Prince is sending a medical convoy here tomorrow," Dr. Sinclair said, her voice a soft hum beneath the steady drip of water leaking through the roof. "They will need local guides, people who know the back roads and the bridges that might be out. Then, they would like us to identify a team to go back to the city with them to help people there." Her eyes, sharp as a scalpel, flicked between Gabriel and Celine. "They could use both of you."

Celine's throat tightened. The taste of ash and desperation lingered at the back of her tongue, memories of the clinic's shattered windows, the blood on bandages, the hollow-eyed children who clung to her sleeves with dirt-caked fingers.

Gabriel's jaw flexed, the muscle jumping beneath his sun-weathered skin.

"And if we go to Port-au-Prince? Who watches our people here in Gonaives?" His voice was like gravel, rough from nights shouting over the roar of floodwaters.

Pastor Claude shifted in the doorway, the wood creaking under his weight. His clothing carried the faint scent of candle wax and damp hymnals. "We'll hold things together."

Mireille and David murmured in agreement, their voices blending with the distant chorus of tree frogs outside.

Dr. Sinclair leaned in, the citrus-and-antiseptic scent of her soap cutting through the heaviness. She turned her gaze toward Celine.

"You have a gift," she said to Celine. "You could attend the National School of Nursing in Port-au-Prince." Then, to Gabriel: "And for you, medical technician training. You both could further your education. I know people."

Celine exhaled sharply, the air tasting of dust and decisions. But beneath the fear, something hotter ignited: purpose.

She caught Gabriel's gaze, the familiar flecks of gold in his dark eyes, the unspoken trust. A barely-there nod passed between them.

"We have to go," she said, her voice steadier than her pulse.

Gabriel's mouth curved, just a ghost of his usual grin, before he turned to Dr. Sinclair and nodded his assent. "I agree," he said.

"Good. We leave at dawn," Dr. Sinclair announced.

PART II

Port-au-Prince

4

New Year's Day

JANUARY 2010

Paper lanterns swayed on rusty wires, casting flickering light over faces filled with anticipation, ready to welcome a new year. Shadows flickered up the walls like unsure flames, revealing hairline cracks in the plaster that no one dared to look at too closely. The smell of burning pork fat lingered in the air, caramelized and greasy, countered by the pungent sweetness of spilled sugarcane juice on a hot grill.

Unaccustomed to revelry, Celine sipped her punch as Gabriel stood stiff as starched linen, his collar scratching at his neck each time he turned, left, right, then left again. The band played a carnival tune, horns blaring with exaggerated cheer. A woman with rugged hands and lavender perfume grasped Celine's wrist and pulled her onto the dance floor. For three breaths, four, Celine let herself go, hips swaying to the rhythm, the familiar lyrics ringing in her head.

At the back of the room, Dr. Sinclair sat perfectly still. The smell of antiseptic still clung to her despite the rum punch sweating in her hand. When the music swelled, her foot tapped, just once, against the uneven floorboards before going still. The trumpet player blew harder. A man spun his wife until her sandals slapped against the concrete. Laughter rose like steam from wet pavement, desperate and evaporating.

Somewhere, deep beneath their feet, the earth shifted in its sleep, as the lanterns flickered, and the cracks in the walls, hidden all evening by trembling light, widened just a little more in the dark.

Tuesday, January 12, 2010, 4:53 p.m.

The earth had always been restless beneath Haiti, a silent beast shifting in its sleep. For centuries, the land had borne the weight of history, colonization, revolution, storms, both political and natural, but it had never entirely broken. But on a quiet afternoon in January 2010, the beast woke up.

There was no warning: no gathering clouds, no whispered prophecies. Just the sun hanging heavy in the sky, the streets buzzing with the usual chaos of a city trying to hold itself together. Markets bustled with bargaining merchants, children darted between motorbikes, and the smell of charcoal smoke filled the air. Then, silence. A breath held too long.

The ground roared.

First came the sound, a deep, guttural growl rising from the center of the world, vibrating through shoe soles and ribcages before erupting into a roar that overwhelmed eardrums. The earthquake's 7.0 magnitude caused the pavement to ripple like liquid, making schoolchildren stumble midstep, their knees scraping against the suddenly soft asphalt. Chalkboards in sweltering classrooms cracked down the middle, their slate splitting beneath the buckling rebar. Around them, buildings collapsed with a roar, folding like wet cardboard, their debris emitting clouds of dust that coated tongues and stung eyes.

In the chaotic days that followed, the air was thick with decay and grief. Haiti, already burdened by poverty and unstable politics, now trembled on its knees, its people tasting salt from tears and dust, their fingers numb from digging, and their ears ringing with the silence that followed each aftershock.

The National Palace collapsed with a deafening crash. The dome's fall sent shards of marble whistling through the air like blades, embedding in palm trees with wet plunks. The gardens, once fragrant with hibiscus and diplomats' cologne, were covered by an avalanche of crushed limestone that coated tongues with the taste of dry bones. Across the street, the Justice Ministry crumbled inward, with each floor collapsing like a snapping spine, concrete dust rising in a mushroom cloud that stung eyes and coated throats with grit.

The dust settled, thick and suffocating. Survivors emerged from the cloud like ghosts, their eyelashes white, their spit turning into gray mud.

Somewhere beneath a pile of cinderblocks, a whimper broke through, then stopped as suddenly as unplugging a radio.

Thirty-five seconds. A lifetime of collapses compressed into one endless moment. And beneath it all, the earth still trembled, not in apology, but warning.

###

And then, the dust, a thick, suffocating haze that turned the sky the color of dried blood. It coated both the living and the dead, blurring the line between them. Screams echoed from the rubble, pleas for help, for water, for a name that would never be answered. The dead were everywhere, tangled in the debris, limbs protruding from concrete like broken branches. The living clawed at the ruins with bare hands, nails splitting against stone, voices raw from calling out to those who might already be gone.

Without order, survival became a tough calculation. Thieves prowled the ruins, stealing watches, wallets, and wedding bands from bodies. The desperate fought over bottles of water and cans of food ripped from broken storefronts. Aid convoys moved slowly through the wreckage, too dispersed and sluggish, their supplies slipping into the hands of the fastest or strongest.

Nightfall brought no relief. The city sank into a darkness so deep it felt like a second burial. Candles flickered in makeshift camps where families huddled under sheets strung between sticks. The air was thick with the smell of sweat, open wounds left to fester, and death that had lingered too long in the sun. Somewhere in the darkness, a mother wailed. Elsewhere, a man whispered prayers over a child who would not wake.

And always, the aftershocks, small, cruel reminders that the earth was still shifting beneath them. Every tremor sent survivors rushing into the open, eyes wide with the fear that the ground would finish what it had started.

###

The sun rose over Port-au-Prince like a fever, hot, relentless, and thick with the smell of burning rubber and wet ash. Twenty yards from the collapsed palace, two teenagers prowled the area near a burned-out car; their curiosity had turned into something sinister. Their fingers tapped restless rhythms on their rifle stocks, eyes darting at every sound. They confronted a biker and stole his gold chains, using them as trade for safe passage through the treacherous streets.

Down the street at the palace ruins, a group of women in torn dresses sifted through the rubble with their bare hands, pulling out splintered chairs, a single shoe, and a photograph. One of them let out a wet, broken sound, not quite a scream, not quite a sob. The prowlers looked away. Further down the alley, the market's corpse had already been stripped clean.

At the crossroads, a pile of tires had burned down to smoldering embers, but the bandits in bandanas were still there, poking the flames with sticks. Their eyes looked too old for their faces. One of them, a girl no older than twelve, threw a broken chair leg into the flames and watched it catch, her face expressionless. The smoke stung her eyes, but she didn't blink.

Nearby, a man in a bloodstained dress shirt argued with a teenager holding a pistol. "That's my truck!" the man shouted.

The teenager shrugged. "Not anymore."

5

After the Quake

JANUARY 2010

P astor Jonathan leaned against the skeletal remains of the St. Francis
School, his shadow stretching long and gaunt across the rubble in the
late afternoon sun. He looked at the list in his hands: seventy-three names
written in the shaky handwriting of exhausted aid workers. Somewhere in
the wreckage, a feral dog snarled over something fleshy and rotten. The
pastor's fingers traced a name halfway down the list: "Sophonie Joseph,
age 8." He remembered her; she was always the first to Sunday school, her
pigtails bouncing as she recited verses with exaggerated seriousness. Now
he dug through concrete dust and splintered desks with his bare hands,
nails splitting against the debris.

"Over here!" Gabriel shouted hoarsely.

Pastor Jonathan scrambled toward the voice, his knees scraping
against the rebar that stuck out from the rubble. Gabriel stood over a cav-
ity in the wreckage. The beam of his flashlight lit up a small hand, palm
up, fingers slightly curled as if still reaching for something. The skin was
gray with dust but not decayed. A miracle or a tragedy; it was getting hard
to tell the difference.

Later, back at the ruins of his church, Pastor Jonathan sank to his
knees. His prayer wasn't whispered in the stained-glass hollow but groaned
through cracked lips. His calloused fingers touched the frayed edges of his
shirt pocket where he kept his private list—names not recorded by any aid
organization.

Marie-Claire. Jean-Luc. Little Samuel, who loved mangoes.

A single tear carved through the dust on his face as distant aircraft lights, another evacuation flight, vanished into the night. Above him, the stars burned with cruel indifference, their ancient light revealing the terrible calculation of disaster: for every set of remains recovered, a family could begin mourning. For every name crossed off the list, a hundred more remained.

The night smelled of smoke, wet cement, and the faintest trace of jasmine stubbornly clinging to life in the courtyard. Somewhere beneath him, the earth still hummed with aftershocks.

The air in the hospital courtyard reeked of the sickly rot of gangrene already spreading in untreated wounds. Celine's dry lips moved silently as she stepped over a puddle of vomit and blood, the two fluids swirling together, still warm beneath her worn-out sneakers.

A child's whimper broke through the groans. Absently, Celine's fingers brushed sweat-soaked curls from the girl's forehead.

Celine's sensory world had narrowed to a mix of intense and conflicting feelings as she treated patients during the aftershocks. The tremors and urgency of the situation triggered a rush of adrenaline, sharpening her focus but leaving her body tense and hyperaware of every vibration beneath her feet. Between the grime, blood, and dust in the air, her hands felt sticky and raw, while the uneven ground beneath her shifted unpredictably, making even simple procedures unnervingly difficult. Finally, a deep, gnawing pressure in her chest, part fear, part determination, as she balanced the immediate needs of her patients with the looming threat of another collapse, knowing every decision mattered.

In the ER, a boy's whimpers cut through the stale air, high, thin sounds like a wounded animal's, barely audible over the clatter of steel trays and the groan of the overtaxed AC unit. The glare of the overhead lights reflected off Dr. Sinclair's glasses as she assessed the boy, his sunken cheeks, the ribs pressing against his threadbare shirt, the grotesque angle of his arm. The clipboard in her hands was a damning ledger: Morphine, low. Sutures, depleted. Beds, full.

Dr. Sinclair sterilized tools in a steaming machine, hurting her fingers on the hot scalpel but ignoring the pain. Nearby, a piece of metal pulled from the rubble seemed to be their only hope. When the boy jerked at the noise of scraping metal, Celine, now serving as a field nurse, comforted him in Haitian Creole, saying, 'You'll be okay, little man,' even though she didn't know the details of that promise.

Despite Celine's fear, she stayed focused and watched Dr. Sinclair set the boy's broken bone with shaky, sweaty hands while his labored breathing matched her racing heartbeat.

When it was over, and the boy finally collapsed from exhaustion, his chest rising and falling in a gentle rhythm, his mother leaned against Celine, her tears soaking through the thin fabric of Celine's scrubs. They were hot, silent, and heavy tears of gratitude.

Celine made her way to the makeshift chapel and dropped to her knees. She no longer asked for miracles. Just for the strength to carry the next body, to whisper the next word of hope.

The stench of infection clung to her scrubs, but her faith never faltered, as she mumbled, "Have mercy, God," under her breath.

Celine remembered the ache in her knees from kneeling on the concrete beside a dying woman, her nose close enough to catch the sour-milk whisper of fear in the woman's breath.

"I'm afraid," the woman mumbled.

Celine's fingers gently held the woman's trembling hands, her knuckles swollen from years of hauling water. She didn't recite Scripture or offer empty words. Instead, her thumbs traced the calluses on the woman's knuckles, her voice as quiet as the hum of the generators outside.

"God sees you. God knows you," she whispered.

Now, kneeling in the chapel, Celine's faith wasn't a lightning bolt from the sky. It wasn't the sudden rush of clean water through broken pipes. Her faith smelled of iodine and sweat; it was sharp, medicinal, human. It lived in the press of her palms as she cleaned an older man's leg ulcer, the wound weeping yellow-green against his ashen skin. It was the scrape of her knees against the floor, the quiet click of her teeth as she ground them against despair. It was the way she still showed up, day after day, her hands raw from washing wounds that might never heal. It was the metallic screech as she pried open a rusted medicine cabinet. The salt of her sweat as she worked through the night, her prayers not whispered but acted, one wound dressed, one bell rung for justice, one trembling hand held until the dawn light washed the ward in pale gold.

Celine remained on her knees, listening. Waiting. Not for a miracle. But for the courage to believe in the next small, stubborn act of mercy.

6

The Collapse of Everything

I n the weeks after the devastating earthquake, the government's operations were severely disrupted as key ministries, hospitals, and administrative buildings were damaged or destroyed. Many officials were among
the dead, injured, or missing, leaving the state apparatus paralyzed. President René Preval's administration struggled to coordinate relief efforts,
relying heavily on international aid organizations and foreign governments
for assistance. The capital, Port-au-Prince, was in chaos, with no centralized system for distributing food, water, or medical supplies.

Political instability worsened as accusations of corruption and
mismanagement surfaced. Critics claimed that government officials di-
verted aid or neglected the most vulnerable populations. The absence of
a functioning judicial system allowed looting and violence to continue
unchecked, while displaced survivors congregated in makeshift camps
with minimal security or sanitation.

The Haitian legislature, already fragile before the disaster, became
even more divided, delaying crucial policy decisions. Elections scheduled
for later in 2010 were postponed, further eroding public trust. Meanwhile,
local leaders and grassroots organizations often stepped in where the government failed, organizing community relief efforts without official back-
ing. Ministers and officials, those still alive, disappeared into the night,
fleeing to guarded compounds or foreign embassies. The police, already

weak, disintegrated; some stayed to help, but many disappeared, knowing they were outnumbered, outgunned, and forgotten.

Into that void, the gangs slithered like floodwater through cracks in concrete. They had always been there, lurking in the slums, but now they moved boldly. Men with rifles and machetes took over the streets, not with subtlety but with fire and force. They claimed neighborhoods as their territory, like kings, setting up checkpoints where they demanded money, food, or loyalty. The few police stations still standing were stripped clean, weapons gone, files burned, walls scarred with bullet holes.

Social services, already fragile before the quake, disappeared completely. Hospitals, where Dr. Sinclair once worked twelve-hour shifts stitching wounds and treating fevers, became overwhelmed with the dying. Records vanished. Medicine ran out. Generators sputtered and died, forcing surgeons to operate by the light of flashlights or candles. The dead piled up outside in the heat, unclaimed, until the stench drove even the desperate away.

In the ruins, Pastor Jonathan's church became a sanctuary. He pushed pews aside to make space for families who had lost everything. He prayed with them, though his voice sometimes quivered, not from fear, but from exhaustion. When gang members arrived demanding "contributions," he stood his ground, even as his hands shook. They laughed at his defiance but left, for now. He knew they would return.

Monique, a schoolteacher with no school to teach in anymore, transformed her small home into a shelter for orphaned children. She fed them whatever she could find, scraps of rice, half-rotted fruit, and told them stories to drown out the gunfire at night. She kept a kitchen knife under her pillow, though she knew it was useless against the men who controlled the streets.

Mark, a mechanic who once repaired tap-taps and motorbikes, lost his livelihood when his workshop was destroyed and buried under rubble. However, he still mended generators for gang leaders in exchange for protection, or at least the illusion of it. He hated himself for doing it, but hunger often overpowered his pride.

Outside the city, in some smaller towns, chaos spread like an illness. Roads were blocked by debris or armed men. Aid trucks were robbed before they could reach the hungry. People who had fled Port-au-Prince, hoping for safety, faced only new dangers, no food, no shelter, no law.

The gangs poisoned what remained of the city's spirit. They went by many names, including G-9 and G-Pep, but all followed the same ruthless rule: control the ruins, control the future. Some pretended to be protectors, distributing stolen aid to gain loyalty. Others ruled through fear, turning ration lines into execution sites and clinics into bargaining chips. Their weapons weren't just guns and machetes but also bureaucracy, ledgers tracking who ate, who lived, and who disappeared.

In the ruins of what was once a city, the people did what they had always done: they survived. Some prayed. Some fought. Some closed their eyes and hoped to wake up somewhere else. But the earth did not listen. And the guns did not stop.

Cholera first appeared in Haiti in October 2010, nearly ten months after the earthquake. The outbreak started in the rural Artibonite region, where contaminated water from a United Nations peacekeeping base introduced the disease into the local river system. From there, it spread quickly across the country, overwhelming Haiti's already weakened healthcare system.

The impact was devastating. Hospitals and clinics, still trying to recover from the earthquake, were overwhelmed with patients suffering from severe dehydration and diarrhea. Many medical facilities lacked adequate sanitation, which further sped up the spread of the disease. Within weeks, cholera reached Port-au-Prince, where crowded displacement camps became breeding grounds for infection.

By the end of 2010, thousands had died, and hundreds of thousands more were infected. The disease disproportionately affected people living in poverty, who lacked access to clean water and medical care. Public anger grew as evidence connected the outbreak to UN negligence, fueling protests and worsening distrust in foreign aid organizations.

The trucks arrived in a cloud of dust, their white panels shining under the sun, marked with acronyms that sounded like alphabet soup on the tongue. They rolled past the collapsed schoolhouse, past the church where bodies still lay buried, and parked behind a line of sawhorses. Men in vests and mirrored sunglasses stepped out, their radios crackling in quick bursts of English, French, and Spanish. Clipboards snapped shut. Doors locked.

Celine watched from beneath a tattered tarp, the nylon sticky against her skin. Five days earlier, a man with a sunburned neck pressed a slip of paper into her palm, Number 217, and told her to return at dawn. She had. The line wound through the ruins, a serpent of hollow-eyed hope. When she finally reached the front, they looked at her ticket and frowned. "Wrong district." The next station had run out of supplies hours earlier.

Nearby, Gabriel spat into the dirt, the glob landing close to a crushed water bottle. The radio crackled again, "rescue operations underway," before fading into static. He knew what was coming. Last week, gray ships appeared on the horizon, their decks loaded with crates. They offloaded ready-to-eat meals, beige pouches stamped with old dates, then raised their gangways like drawbridges. No antibiotics. No sutures. Just vacuum-sealed beef patties that tasted like salt and preservatives.

A murmur moved through the crowd, quiet and urgent: A boat. Tonight. No papers. Just cash. Celine's cousin had disappeared weeks ago, one less mouth to feed, one more ghost to mourn. Or maybe he was in Miami now, drinking water that didn't smell of chlorine and corpses, walking streets that didn't buckle underfoot.

As dusk faded into night, a single bulb flickered on. Beneath its jaundiced glow, Rafael spread out a map, the paper damp with sweat. Exhausted from the suffering, his calloused finger traced a route across the Caribbean, over ink-blue waters where storms gathered and cutters prowled.

"We could try to flee," he said, mostly to himself, though the dangers hung in the air like the smell of the latrines: children lost to the waves, mothers packed into holds like cargo, coast guard spotlights piercing through the darkness. "It's time to escape this wretched hell."

Chicago, Illinois—2010

The community center's basement was thick with the smell of nervous bodies packed too tightly into the small space. The television's blue glow lit up Uncle Pierre's face, casting ghostly shadows on his features. His fingers clenched around the lukewarm mug as Anderson Cooper's somber voice recounted the collapse of the cathedral, federal buildings, and the chaos that followed. Even after some time, the images still triggered sharp jolts through him, like biting down on aluminum foil.

Uncle Pierre wiped his brow with a yellowed handkerchief as the donation basket circulated among community members. He quietly added his rent money with the others, whispering as it dropped. Anderson Cooper's televised voice cut through the chatter as he recounted more bleak details. The earthquake killed an estimated 200,000+ people and displaced millions, making it one of the deadliest natural disasters in recent history.

The radio crackled again: "Mrs. Obama says, 'Text HAITI to donate ten dollars.'"

Roland, one of the community members, spat into the trash can with a wet thud. "Ten dollars? For what? To dig a grave?"

Later, the Western Union office reeked of sweat and ink, with a faint scent of desperation rising from damp money orders clenched in trembling hands. Pierre's fingers left smudges on the yellow form as he wrote, $500 for Celine, the numbers blurring beneath his sweaty palm. Behind the bulletproof glass, the clerk's voice sounded rough, "No guarantees," he said. "The system is down."

Outside, Wyclef's "Yele" blared from tiny iPod speakers, the bass rattling pizza boxes half-filled with crumpled bills. A young white girl in a "Chicago Cares" tank top bounced to the beat, her shoes slapping against the pavement still slick with melted snow. Pierre's tongue burned from the coffee he'd gulped too quickly, bitter, like the irony of charity set to a soundtrack.

The devastating earthquake that struck Haiti on January 12, 2010, tested the limits of international aid and revealed the complexities of U.S.-Haiti relations in real time. Measuring 7.0 in magnitude, the quake reduced entire neighborhoods to rubble, claimed over 200,000 lives, and displaced more than a million people within minutes. The world watched as Haiti, already the poorest country in the Western Hemisphere, faced an unimaginable crisis, one that required a swift and coordinated global response.

The United States, Haiti's closest and most influential neighbor with deep historical ties to the island, responded swiftly. Within hours, President Barack Obama authorized a large-scale emergency operation, deploying over 13,000 military personnel, including Marines and the aircraft carrier USS Carl Vinson, to aid relief efforts. The U.S. military took control of Port-au-Prince's damaged airport, making sure aid shipments could land and supplies could be distributed, an operation that was effective but also drew criticism for prioritizing American logistics over local coordination. Planes filled with food, water, and medical supplies arrived in Haiti, while search-and-rescue teams scoured the wreckage for survivors.

On the policy front, the Obama administration extended Temporary Protected Status (TPS) to Haitian nationals already in the U.S., allowing them to stay and work legally without fear of deportation. The decision was a humanitarian gesture, recognizing that returning people to a devastated country would be unthinkable. However, it was not a blanket invitation; Haitians trying to flee after the quake were intercepted by the U.S. Coast Guard and sent back, a policy that highlighted the delicate balance between compassion and immigration enforcement.

Financially, the U.S. pledged billions in aid, but the flow of money came with conditions. Much of the funding was funneled through American NGOs and contractors, raising questions about whether the assistance truly helped Haitians or increased foreign dependency. Despite good intentions, the relief effort was hindered by bottlenecks, aid piled up in warehouses, reconstruction slowed down, and promises of rebuilding were overshadowed by bureaucracy and corruption. The presence of foreign troops, though initially welcomed, also created tensions, as some Haitians questioned whether the intervention respected their sovereignty.

Historically, the U.S. viewed Haiti through both strategic and humanitarian lenses. American occupation in the early 20th century, Cold War interventions, and shifting support for Haitian leaders built a legacy of distrust, one that the earthquake response did little to improve. The disaster exposed the limitations of disaster capitalism: emergency aid can save lives temporarily, but without real investment in Haiti's institutions, the cycle of instability would persist.

As the dust settled, Haiti was still standing, but just barely. The world's attention drifted away, but the country's struggle continued.

7

Horror Stories of Escape

January 2012

The immediate aftermath of the disaster triggered the first large-scale migration as people fled from collapsed infrastructure, disease outbreaks, and severe poverty that worsened after the quake. Many had lost their homes, loved ones, and sources of income, leaving them with little reason to stay. Over time, as reconstruction slowed and political stability declined, increasing gang violence, government corruption, and economic collapse caused even larger waves of migration. Migrants cited multiple overlapping crises, such as lack of basic security, inability to earn a living, and fear of gang crossfire or kidnappings, as their reasons for leaving.

Haitians began fleeing their country in larger numbers during those years. The first wave of displacement saw many survivors seeking temporary refuge in the neighboring Dominican Republic. Meanwhile, others attempted the more dangerous route to the United States by boat or through Central America.

Those who escaped often had to deal with exploitation from smugglers and strict immigration laws in transit nations. While some received temporary protected status in host countries, many stayed in legal limbo, unable to return home but struggling to establish permanent residency elsewhere.

###

The villagers in Port-au-Prince had heard tales of the American Dream, stories of luxurious mansions, jobs that paid enough to support a family, and schools where children could learn without fear. They also knew of America's proud words: "All men are created." The Declaration of Independence spoke of liberty, the right to pursue happiness. The Constitution laid down the blueprints for justice, tranquility, common welfare, and a government that served the people.

But was that promise intended for them?

For decades, Haiti had been bleeding, initially under dictators, then gangs, and finally disasters that piled up like bodies in a mass grave. By the 1970s and 80s, desperation had hardened into resolve. Some could no longer endure the hunger, the disappearances, or the way armed men controlled the night. If America truly represented freedom, then surely it would open its arms to those fleeing tyranny.

However, when Haitian boat people started arriving on Florida's shores, they were met not with warmth but with handcuffs. Detention centers quickly took them in. Immigration officers reviewed their paperwork, marking them for deportation before they could even present their case. The courts moved slowly, if at all. Meanwhile, Cubans fleeing Castro's regime were welcomed as heroes. They were granted asylum almost automatically under the "wet foot, dry foot" policy, a U.S. immigration policy, in effect from 1995 to 2017, that granted preferential treatment to Cuban migrants. The contrast in the way immigrants were treated was stark and painful.

Some said it was the color of their skin, that America had never truly kept its promises to Black refugees. Others claimed it was fear that Haiti's poverty and instability made its people seem like burdens instead of survivors. Politicians called them "economic migrants," as if desperation made their suffering less real. Laws were manipulated to keep Haitian immigrants out of the U.S.

Still, they came.

In the dim light of a thatch-roofed home, a fisherman named Daniel packed a single bag, a change of clothes, a Bible, and a photograph of his children. His boat was barely more than rotting wood and hope, but if the winds were right, it could carry him to Florida. He had heard stories of those who didn't make it, vessels lost in storms, bodies washing ashore, survivors kept in crowded cells for months. But staying meant watching his family starve or worse. So, he kissed his wife, promised to send money, and pushed off into the dark.

On the crowded deck of another boat, a young teacher named Marie clung to the sides, trying not to feel sick. The smell of sweat and seawater was strong, but what was worse was the fear, knowing that if she were caught, she'd be sent back to the hell she had escaped. Still, she clenched her jaw and held on. America needed to see her, truly see her, not as a problem, but as a person. She had taught children to read even as gunfire echoed outside her classroom. She had buried friends killed for speaking out. If that didn't make her a refugee, what did?

Under the cover of the night, Joseph approached the docks.

"Safe passage... good jobs... only for you, special price," Joseph heard the captain say.

The boat looked like a carcass, bleached wood creaking under its weight, the ribs of its hull splintered where saltwater had eroded through years of neglect. The foul stench of old fish and diesel clung to its planks, blending with the salty morning air that coated Joseph's lips with each breath.

The captain moved through the shadows, his fingers flickering like spider legs in the moonglow. Twenty-seven. Twenty-seven souls pressed against each other in the hull of this rotten vessel, men whose ribs showed through thin shirts, women with babies wrapped too tightly against their breasts, their muffled cries swallowed by the sea's restless churn.

Near the bow, a young man whispered to his wife, "Don't be afraid." His words faded into the whine of the engine turning over. It coughed once, twice, a sound like a man choking on his blood before roaring to life. The vibration rattled through Joseph's soles, shaking loose a splinter that pricked his heel.

Someone heaved as the sharp taste of bile cut through the air. A child whined, then fell silent as their mother pressed a cloth to their mouth. The captain barked something lost beneath the engine's growl, his voice rough as the rope coiled at his feet.

The horizon shifted from black to gray as the first light revealed the rusted cleats and frayed knots of the rigging. The boat groaned beneath them, and for a moment, Joseph wondered if the wood would hold or if the sea would swallow them whole before they ever saw the light of day.

At dawn, the sea was glass, a flat, oily expanse that reflected the pale sky, silent except for the rhythmic slap of water against wood. But by mid-morning, the wind roared to life, dragging its nails across the surface and kicking up white-capped waves that crashed against the hull. The boat groaned, its timbers flexing like old bones pushed too far.

Joseph's knuckles whitened as he gripped the gunwale, his gaze fixed on the horizon, an unbroken line of nothingness, endless and indifferent. The stories echoed like a chant in his mind: boats splitting open like over-ripe fruit, bodies swallowed by the deep before prayers could leave their lips. Coast Guard cutters loomed like steel giants, their engines growling like predators as they herded desperate souls back to the hell they'd fled. Drones hummed overhead, fast boats sliced through the waves, embody-ing the cold efficiency of a system designed to keep them out. Even if the sea spared them, the law wouldn't.

Joseph's breath caught in his chest as the speck sharpened into steel, a Coast Guard cutter slicing through the waves, throwing up sheets of salt spray that glittered like knives in the harsh sunlight. The smell of fear rose from the passengers, sour and electric, blending with the brine-heavy air that coated every gasp.

The boat seemed to hold its breath, wood creaking, ropes snapping tight against the wind, the slow, sickening roll of the deck beneath their feet. It groaned under the weight of too many bodies, twenty-seven where twelve should have been. The ocean air reeked of diesel and fear, the salt spray stinging eyes already raw from exhaustion. A child's quiet sob faded beneath the relentless slap of waves against the rotting hull. Below deck, stagnant bilge water sloshed with the acidic scent of vomit and human waste.

The air was filled with a blinding white light that sliced through the darkness, not lightning, but the searching beam of a Coast Guard cutter.

Chain-link fences rattled in the offshore wind, their clatter drowned out by the growl of idling transport buses. Inside the detention warehouse, heat rose from the concrete floor, seeping through the thin soles of worn-out shoes. A toddler's wail echoed off the aluminum roof as a border agent snapped on latex gloves with a sharp, practiced motion.

"Remove your belts. Remove your shoelaces," he growled.

The commands bounced between languages, neither version offering comfort. Someone's empty stomach gurgled, not from hunger, but from dread. The harsh sting of industrial cleaner fought with the musk of sweat and mildew.

Joseph heard harsh voices from across the room. "We have layered interdiction protocols," the Coast Guard officer said. His gold cufflinks tapped the mahogany table with each word: click, click, click. On the whiteboard, bold black letters spelled out the inevitable: Apprehend. Detain. Remove.

"Policy is policy," the officer sighed, clicking a pen absently.

When Celine first considered studying nursing in the United States, she believed that advanced training would help her improve Haiti's struggling healthcare system. But as she looked into immigration options, she encountered a system complete with barriers specifically designed for Haitians. These barriers revealed America's conflicting attitude toward her homeland: offering just enough opportunity to entice her, but never enough security to help her succeed.

Unlike refugees fleeing state-sponsored persecution, Haitians escaping gang violence and environmental disasters rarely qualified for asylum. U.S. courts consistently rejected their claims, ruling that gang violence, though deadly and widespread, did not count as targeted persecution under immigration law. By the late 2010s, Haitian asylum approval rates had fallen below 30 percent. TPS, granted after the 2010 earthquake, provided temporary relief but no long-term stability. Renewals depended on political changes, leaving families like Celine's in ongoing uncertainty.

The U.S. healthcare system's need for nurses conflicted with its exclusion of Haitian talent. While foreign-trained nurses from the Philippines or India could often transfer their credentials, Haiti's nursing programs lacked American accreditation. Celine had heard about graduates of Haiti's nursing program working as uncertified aides in Miami, their skills going to waste due to bureaucratic hurdles.

Funding her education presented another impossible choice. Denied federal loans and most scholarships, Celine faced international tuition rates, three times those for residents, and risked deportation if her TPS expired. She had heard of peers who were deported mid-degree, stranded with debt and no diploma. Even those who found work faced exploitation: Haitian nurses were 40 percent more likely than U.S.-trained colleagues to work overnight shifts in underfunded hospitals, earning less for the same job.

Haitian migrants who reached America faced systemic disadvantages. They often settled in neighborhoods with underfunded schools, redlined housing, and heavy police presence. Without work permits, many took cash jobs, driving unregistered taxis or cleaning offices, making them vulnerable to wage theft and ICE raids.

Most devastating was the fate of those deported back to Haiti. Planes loaded with migrants were sent to the same gang-controlled neighborhoods they had fled, now marked for extortion as "returnees" with U.S. ties. The American dream for Haitians had become a trap: luring them with the promise of opportunity, only to exile them to even greater danger.

For Celine, the decision was clear but painful. Staying in Haiti meant practicing medicine without enough resources and watching patients die from preventable causes. Leaving meant risking her future within a system meant to exclude her. Her choice would weigh heavily on her regardless, a reflection of Haiti's impossible position in the global order and America's failure to keep its promises and live up to its ideals.

8

The Weight of Freedom

JUNE 2015

The late afternoon sun filtered through the clinic's windows, casting long shadows across the tiled floor. Celine sat across from Dr. Sinclair in her cramped office, her hands folded tightly in her lap. She had rehearsed this conversation in her head countless times.

"You wanted to discuss something?" Dr. Sinclair said, leaning back slightly. Her expression softened as she watched the uncertainty flicker across Celine's face.

Celine took a slow breath. "I need to leave, doctor. Not because I want to abandon Haiti, but because I can't do enough here anymore. Not like this."

Sinclair nodded. She understood. The 2010 earthquake had been only the beginning; each year since had brought more violence, more collapse. Skilled nurses like Celine should have been saving lives, not dodging gang checkpoints on their way to work.

"You've already done so much," the doctor said. "But if you feel you need to go, it should be with a real chance, not risking the journey illegally."

Celine exhaled. "I want to study nursing in the U.S., get my degree. Work with the Haitian community over there. But I don't know how to make it happen."

Sinclair tapped her fingers against her makeshift desk, thinking. She had dealt with enough bureaucratic paperwork for foreign doctors that she had a fairly good understanding of the system.

"There are a few ways," she said carefully. "The first and fastest would be a student visa. If you get accepted to a nursing program, you can apply for an F-1. But you'd have to prove you won't stay in the U.S. permanently after."

Celine frowned. "But I would want to stay. Eventually."

"Which brings us to the next option, a work visa," she said. "Hospitals and universities bring in foreign nurses. You're already trained and skilled. Maybe someone could sponsor you."

She tilted her head. "Would a U.S. hospital hire me before even arriving?"

"That's the problem." She sighed. "Most want you there first. And getting in legally without a job lined up. . ."

Celine's shoulders tensed. She knew of Haitians who had won the green card lottery, but that was pure chance. Others had fled and sought asylum after arriving, but she refused to take that route. She wouldn't lie about why she was leaving.

"What if I apply to schools first?" she murmured.

Sinclair brightened slightly. "That could work." He scribbled something on a pad. "There are programs for foreign-trained nurses. Some even offer scholarships. If you get in, you'll have time to figure out the rest."

Celine smiled faintly, the weight on her chest easing just a little. It wasn't a guarantee, but it was a real chance.

Sinclair studied her expression. "You're good, Celine. Too good to waste here when you could be helping thousands."

She pressed her lips together, emotions swelling in her throat. This wasn't running away. It was repositioning. "Then I start with applications," she said, resolve firming in her voice.

Dr. Sinclair nodded. "And I'll write you whatever letters of recommendation you need."

For the first time in months, hope felt tangible.

A single kerosene lantern flickered between Gabriel and Celine, casting long shadows that quivered with every distant rumble of a passing truck. A dog barked outside, sharp and sudden. Somewhere down the road, a voice shouted, then faded.

Celine turned to face Gabriel. In a straightforward tone, she said, "Dr. Sinclair found a hospital that'll sponsor my student visa. They need Creole-speaking nurses. And my Uncle Pierre has built a support system in Chicago's Haitian community."

Gabriel's hands froze. "You told me you'd never leave."

She pressed her palms flat against the table. "Every day, we pour ourselves into this ground, and it swallows us whole. We've seen disaster piled on top of disaster. What if we're not meant to drown here?"

He finally met her eyes. "And who's left to support those who can't leave? You know who they are. You've seen them, just like I have."

Celine's fingers clenched into fists. "I held a twelve-year-old girl yesterday while she suffered from a rusted nail wound because we ran out of antibiotics. You think I don't feel that?"

Gabriel reached across the table but stopped short of touching her. "Then stay. Help me rebuild the supply lines. The Dominican border is not as tight as . . . "

"And when the next tremor comes?" She suddenly stood up, the lantern light casting shadows on her cheeks. "When the aid stops? Gabriel, everyone is exhausted."

Silence settled between them like dust.

After a long moment, Gabriel leaned back in his chair. "You remember Madame Desir? The one who used to scold us for stealing mangoes when we were kids?" At Celine's nod, he continued, voice rough. "She came to the clinic yesterday. Walked three miles on a broken foot because her grandson had a fever. Who cares for her family if you go?"

Celine turned to the window, where the faint outline of a collapsed building was visible against the starless sky. "You and many other dedicated people can care for those still in need. I can't explain it, but I feel a certain calling to use my gifts in America," she whispered.

After many heartfelt words, Gabriel recognized her deep dedication to a cause bigger than herself and her strong desire to use her gifts and talents for a specific mission. Gabriel nodded once to show he understood her call and that he would support her.

Before she departed, he helped her pack, a single bag holding a change of clothes, her nursing license, and a photograph of them at Carnival, from years ago. At the bus station, he pressed a jar of his mother's peanut butter into her hands. "For the journey," he said.

Gabriel smiled softly, like the morning light, as Celine waved goodbye.

The bus doors hissed shut. Through the smudged glass, Celine watched him get smaller until the turning road swallowed him, just another figure in Haiti's broken landscape, standing firm as the earth itself trembled beneath him.

###

Celine grasped the letter from Dr. Patrice Sinclair, its crisp edges pressing into her palm like a promise. The sponsorship was genuine, a lifeline from one of Haiti's most respected doctors. It marked the first step in a carefully planned strategy: securing a student visa through Dr. Sinclair's influence, Celine's nursing credentials, and the political support of an Illinois congressman who recognized Haiti's urgent need for culturally aware, trained medical professionals.

The government building loomed ahead, its stark white walls and armed guards creating a formidable barrier of bureaucracy. Inside, the air was tense as petitioners waited in nervous silence. Celine's fingers moved carefully over the visa application, slowly filling out the forms. The consular officer, a tired man with ink-stained cuffs, examined her paperwork before giving her a doubtful look.

"Why America?" he asked, his tone devoid of warmth. "Why not stay and help rebuild here?"

Celine sat up straighter, her voice calm despite her pounding heart. "I need the training that only America can provide," she said. "With a proper education, I can do more than patch wounds; I can change entire communities."

The embassy's air conditioning hummed too loudly, its chill causing goosebumps on Celine's skin. The officer tapped her passport; his brow furrowed. "No bank statements? No property ties to Haiti?"

Celine didn't recoil. She had nothing left to offer but the truth. "Everything I owned was buried in the earthquake," she said. "But I have my training, my sponsors, and my word."

The officer exhaled, flipping through Dr. Sinclair's carefully prepared sponsorship packet, pages filled with medical references, the congressman's endorsement, and proof of Celine's acceptance into a reputable Illinois program. His expression softened slightly as he looked over the documents. He turned the pages, stopping at a photograph of Celine in her clinic scrubs, her hands covered with dirt and blood as she worked amid the ruins of the earthquake. When he asked about her experience, she spoke of the makeshift clinic, sterilizing instruments with boiling vinegar, and holding a child's hand as he took his last breath.

"And you'll return to Haiti?" he asked again, as if testing her resolve.

Celine met his gaze. "Every disaster needs survivors who know how to rebuild."

The stamp came down with a decisive thud, the sound of a door swinging open.

As Celine stepped onto the plane, she carried more than just luggage. She held the scent of bleach from the clinic, the weight of Gabriel's flash drive filled with survival tidbits, and the memory of Pastor Jonathan's calloused hands on her shoulders as he prayed. These were her actual credentials, proof of what she had endured and what she aimed to change. America awaited. But Haiti would always remain in her heart.

The plane's engines screamed like living creatures as they lifted the aircraft into the sky. Below, Port-au-Prince shimmered: a mosaic of broken concrete, tin roofs, graves, ghosts, and those who would never escape. The engines roared, drowning out the whimper rising in her throat. Mid-air, she realized her survival wasn't an accident. It was a lesson, shaped by dirty hands, whispered promises, and the unbroken chain of those who had paved the way, clawing toward the light.

The Miami air hit Celine like a damp slap, thick with jet fuel, salt, and the foul smell of overripe fruit from a nearby trash bin. The humidity wrapped around her neck like a noose before she even stepped off the jet bridge. Then came the shock of the immigration hall: an icy blast of air conditioning that made her sweat-chilled skin prickle, accompanied by the sterile smell of industrial cleaner and the sounds of fingerprint scanners. The vinyl floor squeaked beneath her cheap sneakers as she walked, her documents clenched so tightly that the edges left grooves in her palms. The papers smelled of ink and desperation, the sponsorship letters, crisp with hospital letterhead, her university acceptance still faintly chemical from the printer toner.

At the customs counter, the agent's cologne, something sharply citrus, clashed with the sweat beadings at Celine's hairline. His eyes flicked from her Haitian passport to her face with the practiced suspicion reserved for those from places the world would rather forget.

The agent's fingers were as dry as parchment as he took her passport, the plastic cover slightly sticking to his palm. He tapped on his keyboard with deliberate, maddening slowness, each click echoing like a ticking clock.

"Purpose of your visit?"

The words came out more smoothly than she expected: "I'm here to study nursing. At the Westlake University School of Nursing." Her tongue felt thick; she hadn't spoken English in days.

"Never heard of it," he replied.

"It's a small private university on the near west side of Chicago."

His eyebrows lifted. The fluorescent lights hummed overhead, highlighting the silvery stubble along his jaw. "Proof of enrollment?"

She slid the letter across the counter. The paper made a whispery sound against the Formica. He scanned it, then squinted at his monitor, exhaling through his nose, a damp, coffee-sour puff of air.

"No prior U.S. travel?"

"No."

"Who's sponsoring you?"

She recited the name of Dr. Patrice Sinclair. His pen clicked, once, twice, before he spoke.

"Where will you live?"

Uncle Pierre's Chicago address tumbled out, memorized from an email she'd read by flashlight.

The fluorescents buzzed like angry insects as he handed Celine's documents back to her. There was no warm welcome, just the squeak of a rubber stamp on paperwork and the huff of a disinterested bureaucrat.

Her escort stood outside under flickering lights; the humid air was now tinged with the promise of freedom.

"Welcome to America," he said flatly.

Celine slipped her passport into her bag. The cover felt warm to her touch. She was finally here. But the border's fingerprints were all over her.

PART III

Welcome to America

9

In Chicago

SEPTEMBER 2015

A ll of them shared the same hope: that America would be different. That America would save them. But America was not a savior; it was a storm of its own. Airports swallowed them into fluorescent-lit labyrinths where uniformed officers barked questions in a sharp, unfamiliar language. Families were torn apart, parents detained, and children handed over to social workers with exhausted eyes. Those who made it past the gates stepped into a world that refused them. Cities like Miami, New York, and Chicago offered shelter but not protection. Apartments meant for four held twelve; jobs intended for the skilled became sweatshops for the desperate. Wages vanished into the hands of landlords who smirked at their accents and into the pockets of lawyers, who promised miracles for a fee.

And constantly, the threat of ICE loomed at the edges of their lives.

Yet, in the cracks of this unwelcoming world, something stubborn took root. Haitian communities, and similar enclaves, became lifelines. Churches doubled as food pantries, their basements stocked with rice, beans, and powdered milk. Elders held court in crowded apartments, dispensing advice in the familiar cadence of their own homelands. There, they buried their loved ones far from the homeland's soil, but they remained together. They mourned softly in their native tongues, with a hand on a shoulder. They remembered the scents and scenes of their homelands. America had not been the dream they were promised. But they were here. And they would endure.

###

The car smoothly navigated Chicago's streets, with city lights flickering outside the window. Celine sat quietly, her thoughts drifting elsewhere. The escort who picked her up at O'Hare was a man familiar with the Haitian community. As he spoke, he glanced at her in the rearview mirror.

"You've been quiet since we left the airport. First time in Chicago?" The escort asked.

"First time in America," Celine nodded. "It's overwhelming."

The escort chuckled softly. "It always is at first. But you'll find your footing. You're staying with your uncle. Pierre? Correct?"

"Yes," Celine hesitated. "Though I don't remember him well. I met him only twice as a child, despite my parents often talking about him. They said he was a man who never turned his back on anyone."

"That's Pierre. He's been here over thirty years, but his heart's still in Haiti, even if his life's work is here."

"Do you know him well?" Celine asked in a softer voice.

"I know him well enough," the escort replied. "He helped my cousin when she first arrived. He found her a job and made sure she had groceries until her first paycheck. He's like that with everyone. Doesn't matter if you're family or a stranger, if you're Haitian and in need, he'll move mountains for you."

"My parents said the same," Celine responded quietly. "That he left Haiti long ago but never forgot where he came from."

The escort glanced at her again. "He hasn't. He still sends money back and helps with projects there when he can. But his mission's here now, making sure the next generation has a better shot than he did."

"I always wondered why he never went back." Celine folded her hands in her lap. "He could have, once things settled. But he stayed."

"People like Pierre don't leave a fight halfway through." The escort shook his head. "He built something here, networks, support, a community. That's not the kind of thing you walk away from just because it's easier."

"Do you think he resents it? Giving up so much?" Celine asked after a pause.

The escort smiled slightly. "I've never heard him complain. Not once. But that's Pierre. He'll carry the weight without saying a word about it."

The car slowed, turning onto a street lined with three-story walkups. Celine exhaled, her nerves tightening again.

"You'll see for yourself soon enough. He's been waiting a long time to meet you properly."

"I hope I live up to his expectations," Celine said softly.

The escort met her eyes in the mirror, his glance firm but kind. "You already have. Just by being here."

The car pulled to a stop. Somewhere ahead, a light was on, waiting.

###

Celine's days at nursing school began before sunrise.

She woke up at 5:00 a.m. in her small Rogers Park studio, with the hum of the Red Line train already rumbling in the distance. The first light barely touched the sky as she boiled water for coffee, thick, Haitian-style, just like Uncle Pierre had taught her, and reviewed flashcards while eating a quick breakfast. By 5:45 a.m., she headed out the door, walking briskly to the Loyola Red Line station, her backpack heavy with textbooks, her mind already thinking about the day's lectures.

The train ride to the Westlake-Halsted stop lasted 45 minutes if everything stayed on schedule. She used the time to study, her eyes scanning pathology notes or biochemistry diagrams as the city blurred past the window. Sometimes, exhaustion nearly pulled her into sleep, but she fought it; every minute mattered.

By 7:30 a.m., she had reached campus and was heading toward the College of Nursing building. The other students, mostly American-born and many from middle-class backgrounds, were friendly but kept their distance. Some looked at her with polite curiosity, while others did so with subtle skepticism.

"You're from Haiti?" a classmate once asked, eyebrows raised, as if surprised she had made it this far.

"Yes," she replied steadily, refusing to back down. "And now I'm here."

She spoke precisely, her accent softened but still noticeable. She knew some saw her as an outsider, a sponsored immigrant on a student visa, her role in the room uncertain. But she refused to let that define her.

Her visa status loomed over everything. One mistake, like a failed exam or missed deadline, could jeopardize her future. Unlike her classmates, who were born in the U.S., she lacked a safety net. No family in the U.S. could co-sign loans if she ran out of money. No green card guaranteed her place if she faltered.

She worked twice as hard because she had to.

Study sessions stretched past midnight. Weekends were spent in the library, not at bars or parties. She couldn't afford distractions. Sometimes, the loneliness felt overwhelming. She kept in touch with her parents and Gabriel; she saw Uncle Pierre every Sunday, but he couldn't fully understand the pressure of nursing school.

###

As she often did, Celine studied her notes in the student lounge. One day, she barely looked up when she heard the soft squeak of wheels, just another janitor making his rounds. But then the warm, earthy aroma of coffee drifted through the sterile air in the room.

A small paper cup appeared on the corner of her desk.

She looked up to see the old Haitian janitor, his beard streaked with gray; his hospital ID badge frayed at the edges, giving her a faint nod before pushing his cart away. He never spoke, and neither did she. But the following evening, another cup was waiting for her. And the one after that.

One night, as rain tapped against the windows, he stopped by her desk and looked at the diagrams she was drawing.

"You draw well," he said at last, his voice low and gravelly.

Celine hesitated, then slid the notebook toward him. "Anatomy practice."

He examined the page and then pointed to a slightly mislabeled diagram with a finger that was work-roughened. "This one curves more to the side."

She blinked in surprise. "You know anatomy?"

He chuckled. "In another life, I was a medic. Long ago." Then, without saying another word, he pushed his cart down the hall, leaving her staring after him, the coffee steaming between them.

The next day, a well-used notebook appeared beside her usual cup. Inside, detailed handwritten notes, medical terms in French and English, diagrams of procedures, remedies for exhaustion. A lifetime of knowledge, passed silently into her hands.

Celine traced the faded ink and then looked up as the Liberian student from the neighboring cubicle approached her desk.

"He likes you," she murmured, nodding toward the janitor's retreating figure. "Old Etienne doesn't share his notes with just anyone."

Celine didn't respond. But that evening, instead of staying silent, she offered Etienne one of her pastries from the cafeteria; it was a small gesture, a quiet thank you. He took it with a faint smile. And so, their friendship began.

###

The wind at the Westlake-Halsted station didn't just blow; it tore through the air with a relentless, icy hunger. Celine stood on the platform, her coat offering little protection against the late autumn chill. With each breath she took, the air materialized in front of her and almost immediately vanished. The chill pierced her skin, sharp enough to burn her nostrils, carrying the scent of iron from the train tracks and the faint, greasy smell of pretzels warming on a nearby vendor's cart.

Around her, the station buzzed with activity. Backpacks on wheels clattered over uneven concrete, their wheels catching in the gaps between tiles. Voices rose and fell, some hurried, some exhausted, blending beneath the hum of the loudspeaker announcing departures. The scarf wrapped around her ears muffled the noise, enveloping her in a cocoon of wool and her thoughts.

She shifted her weight from one foot to the other, her boots softly tapping the ground. A train rumbled in the distance, its approach vibrating through the platform, but it was not her train. Not yet.

Nearby, a couple huddled together, their laughter bright against the gray afternoon. A man in a heavy overcoat checked his watch, then sighed, his breath blending into the fog in the air. Celine tucked her hands deeper into her pockets, her fingers curling for warmth.

The wind gusted again, sharper this time, and she turned her face away, letting the scarf shield her. The sounds of the city, the sounds of waiting, all of it surrounded her as she stood there, bracing against the cold and counting down the minutes until the train arrived.

10

No Friendly Welcome

OCTOBER 2016

After a year in nursing school, Celine realized that the respected halls of academia favored some students more than others. For these strangers in a foreign land, each day brought new challenges. They moved across campus like ghosts, present but invisible, speaking but unheard. Their accents revealed them as outsiders before they could even act. Local students quickly formed friendships through shared cultural understanding, while international students remained on the fringes, sometimes becoming the subject of jokes.

In lecture halls meant for native speakers, professors' words sometimes slipped away like water. Each classroom discussion was a test not only of knowledge but also of language comprehension and cultural insight. Office hours became confessional booths where pride went to die, as students admitted week after week that, once again, they hadn't quite understood.

The bureaucratic maze was just as challenging. Visa rules loomed over every decision like a swinging sword; missing a class, failing a course, or making a mistake with paperwork made them feel like they were just one step away from disaster. Financial pressure weighed heavily from every side, with tuition costs leaving families back home struggling, and work restrictions offering no legal way out. Some took risks they never would have considered back home; all of this was done just to get by in this land of supposed opportunity.

Homesickness was a constant companion, surfacing at the worst times. A whiff of familiar spices from a passing restaurant. A holiday they couldn't celebrate. A call home interrupted by static. These small sorrows piled up like snowflakes, each one barely noticeable until they created an avalanche of longing.

What kept them going? The same thing that first brought them here: that stubborn, foolish, beautiful belief that it would all be worth it in the end. That sacrifices would turn into something tangible and that their families' investments would pay off. One day, they might look back on these struggles as necessary growth rather than wasted tears. Their story was about late nights, calculated risks, cultural misunderstandings, quiet wins, and the incredible resilience of ordinary people chasing education across borders.

The faint glow of Celine's laptop screen cast shadows across her face as she hunched over her kitchen table, her fingers trembling above the keyboard. Outside, the Chicago wind rattled the windowpanes, matching the unease rattling in her chest. The email on the screen stared back at her.

"Failure to comply with visa documentation requirements may result in termination of your SEVIS status."

Her phone buzzed loudly against the table, Uncle Pierre calling again. She didn't want to answer, didn't want to admit she might have ruined everything. But on the third ring, she exhaled sharply and grabbed it.

He spoke with urgency. "Celine, I've been trying to call you. Why didn't you answer? You're worrying me," Pierre's deep voice rumbled through the receiver. "Tell me what's happening."

Her throat tightened. "I think I messed up," she whispered. "The university says I didn't turn in the right papers, and the ones I submitted were not on time. They're saying," her voice cracked. "They're saying I could lose my visa."

A heavy silence filled the room. Suddenly, Marcus's sharper, closer voice shattered the quiet and joined the call on the speaker. "Wait, what? Let me come over. Right now." Marcus was a family friend and also a nursing student at Westlake. He must have been at Pierre's apartment. She could picture them exchanging grim, protective, angry looks.

Twenty minutes later, Marcus pushed open her door, his windswept dreadlocks and easy grin replaced by a frown. Celine clutched a folder full of papers. Without a word, she set it down on the table and opened it.

Uncle Pierre growled as he scooted his chair closer to the table. "Show me every email. Every notice. All of it."

Celine's hands trembled as she checked the messages. "The first one said I needed to verify enrollment, but the wording was confusing. I thought I had until the end of the month, but I guess not." She swallowed hard. "It was due last month. And then I sent the wrong form because it didn't specify which one to use!"

Marcus hissed through his teeth. "And when you called the office?"

"Well, the woman kept saying, 'The system shows noncompliance,' as if I were some kind of criminal," Celine muttered, pressing her hands against her eyes. "Then she said, 'This is why we have to be strict now.' Like I was trying to cheat the system!"

Pierre's jaw clenched. "They treat every mistake like a major offense."

Marcus paced by the window, restless. "I had a friend last year, Haitian too, who got a parking ticket and didn't realize it was a state fine, not city. Next thing he knew, ICE was questioning him over failure to follow U.S. laws." He shook his head. "They want us to slip up."

Celine's breath quickened. "I just wanted to study. To become a nurse. But now I might have ruined it." Her voice dropped to a panicked whisper. "What if they deport me?"

Pierre slammed his fist on the table, not out of anger at her, but at the invisible forces tightening around them. "No. We fix this." He jabbed a finger at the papers. "We go back to that office tomorrow, together, and we make them explain, line by line. And if they won't listen?" He pulled out a business card with the title Chicago Immigrant Advocacy Network printed on it and slid it toward her. "Then we bring in people who will make them listen."

Marcus squeezed her shoulder. "You're not alone in this, my friend. We won't let them scare us out of our futures."

For the first time in weeks, Celine felt her lungs exhale tainted air. The fear was still there, gnawing at her ribs, but so was something else, a spark of defiance.

She examined the card, then looked at her uncle and friend. "Okay," she said, straightening her shoulders. "We make them explain everything. And we fight."

Outside, the wind kept howling. But inside, the three of them huddled over the paperwork, their voices blending with determination into the night.

The bright lights of the Chicago immigrant rights center flickered overhead as rain hammered against the windows, and the murmur of conversations in various languages filled the air. Celine sat at a busy table, her fingers nervously tapping on the student visa forms spread out before her, and a tight knot formed in her stomach. One incorrect checkbox, one missing signature, and the threat of losing her university status, and possibly facing deportation, could become a reality.

Marcus slouched beside her, flipping through a packet, while Pam, a volunteer from the center with short copper curls and a no-nonsense smile, leaned forward, marker in hand. "Okay, Celine, let's tackle this together," she said, underlining a section. "This is the form you need, not the one they first gave you. Classic bureaucratic mix-up, happens all the time."

Celine exhaled slowly. "At the international office, they made it seem like I just wasn't paying attention," she said, frowning. "Like I was the problem."

Marcus scoffed. "Nah, their system's designed to confuse people on purpose. Remember Jamal? Got his renewal denied last year because the website glitched mid-application, and they refused to admit fault." He shook his head. "You've got to have someone who knows their game."

Pam nodded, jotting down notes. "We see this every week. Universities panic about federal compliance and start blaming students instead of fixing their own messes." She slid another sheet forward. "Now, here's the good news: we can submit a corrected packet with a cover letter from us explaining the miscommunication. That usually stops the clock on any penalties."

Some of the tension in Celine's shoulders eased. "So, it's not too late?"

"You're not alone in this," Pam said firmly. "Legal limbo is their favorite intimidation tactic, but knowledge is your armor. We'll make sure you're covered."

Across the room, a door swung open, and a group of students flooded in for an evening workshop, their chatter filling the space. Pam motioned for Marisol, one of the volunteers, to come over. A petite woman with round glasses, Marisol listened intently as Pam explained Celine's plight. "Hey! We've got a support group starting in a few minutes," Marisol assured Celine. They're students dealing with precisely this kind of stress. You should join."

Marcus nudged Celine's foot under the table. "Go. I'll finish helping Pam with this paperwork. Haitian stubbornness runs deep. We're not letting some clerical error ruin your future."

Celine hesitated before standing up, smoothing her sweater. The fear still lingered, whispering at the edges of her mind: "What if it's not enough?" But as she moved toward the circle of students sharing stories, their voices warm and their nods understanding, something shifted.

Amina, from Nigeria, gently tapped the seat beside her. "They told me my scholarship was canceled because of a 'system error' too," she murmured as Celine sat down. "I slept in the library for a week, afraid to even check my email. But the center fought for me, and won."

One by one, the others shared stories of professors who believed they couldn't speak English, landlords who demanded extra deposits, and the ongoing feeling of being seen as a liability rather than a person. However, they also shared victories, including overturned decisions, reinstated scholarships, and protest campaigns that led to policy changes.

Marisol passed around steaming cups of tea. "This system wants you to feel small," she said, stirring honey into hers. "But you're not just one student fighting alone. You're part of a tide."

Celine wrapped her hands around her cup, feeling the warmth seep into her skin. For the first time in months, the future didn't seem like a narrowing tunnel; instead, it felt like something she could shape, with the right tools and the right people.

When she returned to the table, Pam was sealing an envelope with a satisfied grin. "Done. We'll hand-deliver this tomorrow, with a strongly worded memo about their 'processing errors.'"

Marcus high-fived her, then draped an arm around Celine's shoulders. "See? Told you they've got your back."

The rain had ceased. Outside, the wet pavement glistened under the streetlights, mirroring the glow of the center's windows, bright against the Chicago night.

Celine smiled. The fight wasn't over. In the future, she would have to pay closer attention. Knowledge would be her power.

###

The student study lounge was a peaceful refuge amid the chaos of nursing school, stacks of textbooks scattered across scratched tables, the sharp chemical scent of dry-erase markers mixing with the earthy aroma of microwave snacks. Celine dropped into an empty chair beside Rosita, her nursing textbook hitting the table with a loud thud that echoed throughout the room.

Marcus looked up from his notes, his usually bright eyes shadowed with fatigue. "You look like you just lost a fight with pharmacology," he said, nudging a caramel candy toward her.

Celine sighed, unwrapping the candy and letting the sweetness melt on her tongue. "I feel like I lost a fight with pharmacology. And microbiology. And the entire concept of sleep."

Amina leaned forward, her braids slipping over one shoulder. "We all do," she murmured. "But there's more than that bothering you. What is it?"

The room seemed smaller. Celine ran her finger along the edge of her textbook, its corners worn from endless flipping, before speaking. "Clinicals start next week," she said. "What if I freeze up? What if they decide I don't belong?"

Paulette, who had been quiet, tapped her fingers on her coffee cup. "They already think we don't belong," she said bluntly. "Ever notice how they re-explain things to us like we missed it the first time? But when Taylor or Jake from down the hall messes up, it's 'Oh, everyone makes mistakes!'"

Rosita rolled her eyes and popped a handful of pretzels into her mouth. "My goodness, yes. Last week, Dr. Patel interrupted me during rounds to correct my pronunciation of 'femoral artery,' but when Derek called it a 'leg vein,' no one batted an eye."

The group burst into tired laughter, the kind that comes from recognizing a frustration too familiar to be shocking anymore.

Amina exhaled, swirling her tea. "Back home, mistakes were simply lessons. Here? They seem like proof we shouldn't have come."

A heaviness filled the air, not only from the exhaustion of exams, but also from the unspoken pressure of visas and scholarships hanging by a thread, knowing that one misstep could undo everything.

Then Rosita reached out and squeezed Celine's hand. "Look, we've already survived worse than many people," she said. "Remember that microbiology final where the fire alarm went off twice? And we still passed."

Felicia smirked. "Or when Marcus gave an entire presentation on cardiac arrest protocols with his scrubs inside out, "

"That," Marcus interjected, pointing a finger, "was a deliberate fashion statement."

Celine burst into laughter, easing the tension. Around her, the group's teasing and exaggerated groans filled the room, Amina sharing her disastrous first IV attempt, Paulette's reaction when she realized she'd worn her badge upside down for a week.

For a moment, it wasn't about proving themselves or the constant fear of being seen as unfit to stay. It was just them, students who had cried over textbooks together, shared instant noodles at 3 a.m., and recognized each other's tells when exhaustion turned into frustration.

Celine let her shoulders relax. The mountain of expectations hadn't gotten any smaller. But the weight was easier to carry when it wasn't hers alone.

Marcus stretched his arms wide, grinning. "Alright, enough trauma bonding. Who's up for a late-night diner run? I need pancakes to recover from this emotional vulnerability."

And just like that, the fear didn't vanish, but the path forward felt a little less lonely.

###

Marcus dropped his backpack with a thud that shook the table, causing Rosita's carefully organized pharmacology flashcards to scatter into disarray. "They're auditing all international students in clinical rotations," he announced, flicking an email on his phone toward the center of the table. The university logo stared back at them, followed by the words Compliance Review in bold red.

Amina leaned forward. "What's the catch this time?"

"Updated policy." Marcus tapped the screen. "Now they want our on-call schedules cross-checked with ICE's enhanced monitoring database."

The lead in Paulette's mechanical pencil snapped with a sharp crack. Tiny shards of graphite scattered across the table like shrapnel. "Let me guess, another 'administration error' when they conveniently lose someone's paperwork?"

Rosita's gold bangle clinked against the table as she reached for her phone. "My cousin at UIC got flagged because her bus pass showed 'suspicious travel patterns'; she works night shifts at a pediatric clinic in Pilsen twice a week." Her voice stayed steady, but her fingers trembled slightly against the device.

A pit formed in Celine's stomach. She could still hear the international office adviser's clipped tone from that morning: "Your clinical hours don't match our records." Never mind that the hospital's scheduling system had been glitching for weeks. Never mind that she had submitted fourteen correction forms. The threat had been apparent in the way the woman kept touching the Denial of Status Appeal pamphlet on her desk.

During their study session on Thursday evening, another email arrived, buried under university spam, about parking permits and dining hall surveys. The subject line caught Celine's eye: "Pilot Program: Student Advocacy Hub: Your Feedback Requested." She skeptically clicked it and then called the others over.

There it was: a proposed centralized portal to track administrative delays, financial aid, enrollment, and visa compliance, all in one place, with assigned case managers and clear deadlines for resolutions.

Rosita leaned in, scrolling. "This looks like what we kept saying they needed," she murmured. Marcus snorted. "Yeah, or it's just another 'we hear you' PR stunt."

But Amina lingered on the phrase 'escalation paths.' Last semester, she had spent weeks pleading with the International Office to fix a clerical mistake that threatened her visa. "What if there was a rule," she wondered aloud, "that required them to respond within ten days?" Paulette nodded, recalling the endless cycle of calling three departments only to be told, "Not our problem."

The group grew silent, staring at the mocked-up dashboard. It looked almost naïve in its promise, a digital lifeline in a system tangled with red tape. Still, the pilot program was looking for testers and feedback. Celine cracked her knuckles. "Worth a shot," she said. "Before one of us gets deported over a typo."

The email didn't answer everything, but it was a start. Celine, Amina, Paulette, Rosita, and Marcus looked at the proposed "Student Advocacy Hub" with a mix of hope and exhaustion.

As they reviewed the proposal, they tapped their pens and furrowed their brows. They selected Celine to be the scribe for their brainstorming session.

Celine began to type a draft of their response: "We appreciate the initiative, but the portal needs to be more comprehensive. Like, what happens if financial aid exceeds the ten-day deadline? Does it automatically alert a dean?"

Marcus leaned over the screen. "Yes! And add that international students can't afford to 'wait and see' because visa issues escalate fast. We need guaranteed priority review for anything related to our visa status."

Rosita's response was quiet but firm. "The case managers should have to meet us face-to-face if an issue isn't resolved in two follow-ups. No more hiding behind 'We're experiencing high volumes.'"

Paulette leaned back in her chair and crossed her arms. "The feedback ratings can't just vanish into a report no one reads. We should demand quarterly public statistics, such as the fact that 85 percent of international students waited over three weeks for visa clearance. The stats might shame them into caring."

Marcus, always the joker, grinned. "And end with something like, This pilot will be a complete failure if it simply automates the runaround. Make it polite. You know. But spicy!"

Celine paused her note-taking. "Perfect. I'll type up the final draft. We'll copy the International Student Office and the Dean. Make sure they know that we're watching."

The group exchanged glances. For once, it felt less like shouting into the void and more like laying down a gauntlet.

"Now we wait," Amina added softly.

None of them knew if their suggestions would be considered seriously, but as nursing students, they understood this much: when systems fail, you don't wait for permission to stop the bleeding. At the same time, they shared a sense of foreboding, afraid there might be retaliation for their boldness.

11

Where's Marcus?

The Alarm, 5:30 a.m.

The buzz of Marcus's phone shattered the darkness. He groaned and rolled onto his side, the sheets damp with sweat despite the Chicago winter sneaking through his thin apartment walls. His hand reached out to silence the alarm. For a moment, he lay there, staring at the ceiling and listening to the hum of the radiator as it fought against the cold.

"Five more minutes," he murmured, still half asleep.

But what was supposed to be five minutes turned into ten, and he forced himself to his feet. The floor was icy beneath his bare feet. He flicked on the light, squinting against the sudden brightness. His studio was small, just a twin bed, a desk buried under textbooks, and a mini-fridge humming in the corner. A single framed photo sat on the nightstand: his mother, back in Port-au-Prince, smiling in the sun.

The Run, 6:00 a.m.

The cold air hit him like a slap as he stepped outside. He pulled his hood up, breath fogging in front of him as he started his morning run. The streets were quiet, with only an occasional delivery truck passing by. He ran along the lakefront, the wind biting at his face, and the steady, deliberate rhythm of his sneakers hitting the pavement.

Running was the one habit he'd kept from before. Back then, it was about survival, sprinting through alleyways, dodging bullets, and outrunning rivals. Now, it's just about clearing his head before another day of clinicals and exams.

The Coffee Shop, 7:30 a.m.

He stopped at La Colombe, the same place every morning. The barista, a tired-looking woman named Rosa, already had his usual black coffee, no sugar, ready.

"Long night?" she asked, sliding it across the counter.

"Always," he muttered, handing her a crumpled five.

He sipped the coffee as he walked, the heat seeping into his fingers. His phone buzzed, a message from Celine, his study partner.

"Are you alive? Pharm exam in two hours."

He typed back: "Barely. Meet you in the library."

The Library, 8:00 a.m.

The Westlake University library was already half-full when he arrived, with students hunched over laptops and nursing scrubs wrinkled from overnight shifts. Celine was at her usual table, her dark hair piled into a messy bun, highlighters scattered across the desk.

"You look like hell," she said as he dropped into the chair beside her.

"Feel like it." He pulled out his pharmacology notes, rubbing his eyes. He'd been up until 2 a.m. memorizing drug interactions, only to wake up three hours later.

She slid a granola bar toward him. "Eat something before you pass out."

He tore into it, barely tasting it.

The Exam, 10:00 a.m.

The test was brutal. Marcus's hand cramped halfway through, his mind foggy from lack of sleep. He knew the material; he had to learn it, but the numbers and side effects blurred together.

"Focus."

He forced himself to breathe, to slow down. He wasn't in Port-au-Prince anymore. He wasn't running from anything. He was here. He was safe.

The Hospital, 12:30 p.m.

After the exam, he headed directly to his shift at Memorial. He changed into scrubs in the locker room, with the fluorescent lights worsening his headache.

"Marcus, you're with me today," Nurse Patel said, handing him a chart. "Room 412, post-op. Vitals every hour."

Marcus nodded, switching into work mode. The hospital was his safe place, the beeping monitors, the smell of disinfectant, and the way patients looked at him like he was someone who could help them.

For eight hours, he moved from room to room, checking vitals, adjusting IVs, and listening to elderly patients talk about their grandkids. It was exhausting, but it felt good. It was the life he had fought for.

The Invitation, 9:00 p.m.

Marcus was halfway home when his phone buzzed again. Jean.

"Bro, are you working tomorrow?"

Marcus sighed. "No. Why?"

"Come out. Holiday party at Paradise Lounge. You study too much."

He hesitated. He had a mountain of reading to do, but the thought of spending another night alone in his apartment, staring at the same notes, made his chest tighten.

"Fine. One drink," he muttered, patting his back pocket out of habit. The ridge of his student ID pressed against his fingers through the leather. Safe. Legal. Fine."

###

Inside the club, the air was heavy with sweat and cologne; bodies pressed close under strobe lights. Jean immediately spotted him, slinging an arm around his shoulders.

"Look who decided to live a little!"

Marcus forced a smile, letting himself be pulled into the crowd.

For the first time in weeks, he wasn't thinking about exams or hospital shifts or the past.

The bass from the speakers made Marcus's teeth vibrate. He pressed his soda glass to his forehead, letting the condensation cool his skin. Nursing textbooks sat in his backpack by the coat check, but Jean had sworn this would be "just one drink."

Across the bar, a group of Haitians held court, their laughter cutting through the music. Marcus recognized the cadence, that particular Port-au-Prince bravado worn by men who had left but hadn't escaped.

"Marcus! What, nurses don't dance?" Daniel appeared beside him, reeking of rum. His pinky, missing since the La Saline raid, hooked around Marcus's belt loop.

###

Chicago's winter cold clung like a second skin as Marcus stumbled into the alley to get some air. Jean followed, gleefully recounting some political scandal back home.

Marcus froze. Three black SUVs glided soundlessly around the corner. No sirens. No lights.

His body reacted before his brain. "Jean, go."

Doors burst open. "ICE! Hands where we can see them!"

A flashlight beam pinned Marcus against the wall. His wallet, with his Westlake student ID and F-1 visa, burned in his back pocket.

"Well, well." Agent Richmond stepped into the light, his smile glinting. "Marcus Antoine. We met at that protest last April, didn't we?"

The handcuffs grew tighter as Marcus watched the club's neon sign flicker.

Agent Richmond flipped through the confiscated wallet. "Westlake Nursing, huh?" He held up the student ID like a dirty rag. "Funny. Our system says you're G-9 affiliated."

"That's not true."

A knee jammed into his spine. "Save it." They threw Marcus into the back of the SUV.

As they turned onto I-90, Marcus closed his eyes. In his mind, he was back in Port-au-Prince, the iron, the gunpowder, the gang lieutenant's voice: "No matter how far you run, brother, we own you."

###

Celine kept glancing at the empty seat beside her. Her fears grew worse when Paulette slid into the row, looked around with her mouth in a tight line, and whispered, "Where's Marcus? His housemates said they hadn't seen him since yesterday."

Celine's stomach dropped. Marcus had told her he was going to meet a friend for drinks in River North. As the classmates looked more closely into the case, the pieces began to click. They discovered information about the ICE arrest at the Paradise Lounge. Someone sent Amina a livestream of the incident. Her hands quivered as she watched the footage, flashing lights, shouting, bodies pressed against plexiglass. And there, in the chaos, Marcus's locs swung as he was pushed into a van, his mouth open mid-protest.

Celine's throat burned as she watched. Not him. Not like this.

Philippe Jean-Louis smelled of ink and deodorant soap when he cornered Celine outside the community center the next day. His pressed shirt contrasted with the exhaustion under his eyes. "You're Marcus's friend," he said, more of a statement than a question, flipping open a notepad. "Tell me about him. Not just the arrest, him."

Celine bristled. "You want a sob story for your article? His favorite color was orange. He hated cilantro. He has been in school for the past two years and has been working extra shifts to finish his nursing degree. Now what?"

Philippe didn't balk. "I want to know why a nursing student with no record was flagged for deportation after a bar check." He pulled out a document from his bag and handed it to Celine, the detention transfer order. "They're moving him to Miami tomorrow. I understand that no lawyer was present when he was processed."

The paper shook in Celine's grip. Philippe's fingers brushed hers as he steadied it, and she glimpsed a silver bracelet under his cuff, a Saint Michael medal, just like her grandma wore.

As her anger eased, Celine noticed Philippe's Haitian heritage in subtle details, the kind that whispers rather than shouts. When he spoke, it was clear, a gentle rhythm in his vowels that reflected the language of home, warm and deliberate. His laugh, deep and resonant, rolled like waves on a shore, unhurried and full-bodied. The cadence of his speech captivated her.

Then there were his hands, elegant and precise, as they gestured while he spoke. The way he absentmindedly adjusted the woven bracelet on his wrist, its blue and red threads frayed but still vibrant, was a quiet statement. When he leaned in to listen, his expression changed, a flicker of recognition at certain words and a subtle tightening when politics came up, the kind of tension only someone with Haitian roots would carry so lightly. And beneath it all, lingering on his clothes was the faintest hint of spice, something smoky and peppery, like an echo of a home-cooked meal.

"You have roots in Haiti, don't you?" Celine stated, rather than asked. Some things were known.

"You're right. But my people have been here for decades," Philippe responded.

###

The cafe on Devon Avenue smelled of buttered pastries, with the hum of conversation blending with the clatter of plates. Celine sat by the fogged-up window. Outside, Chicago's January wind tore through the sidewalks, but inside, the air was thick with unspoken tension.

Philippe slid into the booth across from her, his coat covered with melting snow. His face was carefully neutral, but his fingers tapped a shaky rhythm against the table, impatience or nerves, she couldn't tell. He had asked for this meeting, saying he wanted to understand. But understanding, Celine knew, was only the first step.

"You said you had something to tell me," Philippe started softly.

She observed him; the way he dressed was tidy and deliberate, with a crisp shirt and sleeves rolled up against the chill, as if he carried memories of warmer breezes. He had the air of a man who moved through the world with confidence and a sense of belonging. She leaned forward, the vinyl seat creaking beneath her. She told him about Marcus.

Celine's parents had known Marcus' grandmother. Marcus grew up in the crowded, sunbaked streets of Port-au-Prince, where poverty clung to every corner like dust. His childhood was a patchwork of hunger and resilience, a one-room home with a rusted tin roof, meals that depended on his grandmother's limited earnings, and the constant hum of struggle just outside the door. The gangs controlling the neighborhood had always been there, lurking like shadows, promising false protection and belonging. By the time he was fourteen, their influence had become too strong. Desperation forced him to make a choice: he joined them, trading pieces of his innocence for survival.

Even during those years, he carried a quiet gentleness, an attentive way of listening, and a reluctance to raise his fists unless pushed to the limit. His grandmother had instilled that kindness in him; her voice was gentle yet firm as she told him, "You're better than this." When she died suddenly, feverish and in a clinic with too few medicines, something inside him broke, and the gangs no longer felt like refuge; they became just another kind of prison.

So, he ran. Not all at once, but slowly, carefully, scraping together odd jobs, avoiding old loyalties until he found a lifeline: a scholarship to study nursing in Chicago. Leaving Haiti felt like stealing a future he wasn't supposed to have. In America, he clung to his purpose with both hands. He memorized medical terms until his brain was tired, volunteered at clinics, and learned to smile again. His professors called him diligent; his patients called him kind. His friends called him the life of the party.

That's why the deportation notice didn't make sense. He had built a life on second chances, followed every rule, and even allowed himself to dream of opening a clinic back home someday. But the system didn't care about redemption. It only saw the boy he had been, not the man he'd fought to become.

The steam from Philippe's coffee curled between them as she spoke. He didn't interrupt, but his posture shifted, shoulders sinking slightly, as if her words carried weights.

For the first time, Philippe looked at Celine with sympathy. "I understand," he said. He exhaled slowly and deeply. "What do you want me to do?"

It was the first real question he'd asked her.

Celine nodded and allowed herself a small, tired smile. She signaled the waiter for two fresh coffees. The gesture was subtle, yet it carried significant meaning. They were about to discuss strategy now. They were preparing for a fight.

12

Almost Finished

April 2018

C eline's hands still trembled as she arrived at Uncle Pierre's grocery store. The crumpled letter from the Illinois Board of Nursing pressed in her hand as she pushed open the door, the bell ringing loudly overhead. Behind the counter, Pierre saw her face and immediately reached for the bottle of rum he kept for emergencies.

"Tell me," he said, pouring two fingers into a coffee mug.

She slid the letter across the counter. The words stared back at them like an indictment: "Discrepancies in educational documentation. Investigation pending. Clinical privileges suspended."

Pierre's jaw tightened. "What discrepancies?"

Celine exhaled sharply. The nursing school she had attended in Port-au-Prince was destroyed. Her transcripts existed only as water-stained copies, signed by Dr. Sinclair. The board wanted the originals. Originals that no longer existed.

Uncle Pierre read the letter once, then again, as if he thought the words might rearrange themselves. "This is deliberate," he said finally. "They're looking for any excuse to push you out."

Celine realized he was right. Her throat burned. Without graduating, her visa would expire. Everything, the sponsorships, the sacrifices, the unspoken promise to use her gifts to help her people, was hanging by a thread.

Celine clutched the letter that demanded "additional proof of residency." No such request had been made of the Polish boy next door,

78

whose mother baked paczki that filled the hallway with the scent of fried dough and jam.

"We have to be careful," Uncle Pierre said, his smile stretching tight as a rubber band. "So many records were lost or falsified after the earthquake."

The taste of Uncle Pierre's buttery pastries, usually warm and comforting, dissolved into dust in Celine's mouth as she sank into her chair. Philippe sat across from her. The usual steadiness in his dark eyes had been replaced by something harsher and heavier.

"Celine," Philippe said softly, "we need to talk about what happens next. If your student visa is revoked, you'll have to return home. End of story. But what if you wanted to stay?"

She placed her stethoscope on the table between them, the shiny metal catching the faint kitchen light. "I already know the steps. Status adjustment. Green card, waiting period, naturalization."

Philippe exhaled sharply. "It's not that simple." His fingers moved restlessly, tapping the table, adjusting his glasses, as if he could physically rearrange the truth into something easier. "When they investigate, they won't just check your papers. They'll dig. They'll call your university, demand transcripts, and interview your professors."

Celine frowned. "I have nothing to hide."

"That doesn't matter." His voice cracked slightly, the calm reporter's tone slipping. "If they find any discrepancy, any tiny thing, they'll call it fraud. They'll issue a Notice to Appear. You'll have to stand in front of a judge who doesn't care how many lives you've saved."

Her fingers tightened around her stethoscope. "The agency in Port-au-Prince handled everything legally. I didn't forge anything."

"Celine." His hand twitched as if he wanted to reach for hers, but he stopped himself. "The law doesn't care about your intentions. It only cares about their interpretation."

A siren wailed outside, its sound drowned out by the Chicago wind. "What if it goes wrong?" Philippe's voice was barely audible now. "If they deport you, the headlines will call it justice. If you stay, they'll call it a loophole that needs to be closed."

Celine let out a slow breath. Philippe reached across the table, not for the paperwork, but to gently press his palm over hers. "You don't have to do this alone," he said.

"Okay," she said softly. "Then tell me what we do next."

And for the first time that night, she breathed.

The busy hum of the community center surrounded them like static. Each volunteer's fingers moved with practiced rhythm, flipping, stacking, aligning, until the pamphlets formed neat towers on the folding table. "Know Your Rights" stared up at her in bold font. The ink smelled sharp, chemical, sticking to her skin like the antiseptic of hospital corridors.

Celine took a seat at the work table and began to help with the project. Sitting beside her, Philippe leaned in, his elbow grazing hers. She could feel his warmth and smell the faint cedar scent of his soap lingering on his skin.

"So, you will finish nursing school in May 2019, if everything goes as planned. Correct?" he said, tapping his pen against the paper. A habit. A tell. He was nervous for her. "What then?"

She didn't look up. A rogue staple pierced her thumb, and she absentmindedly pressed the small bead of blood away. "I stay." Simple. Defiant. In that moment, she realized she couldn't go back to her homeland. She had lost her place there. Besides, there was too much work to do here.

Philippe exhaled through his nose, a quiet, frustrated sound. "The F-1 visa is a tightrope," he murmured. "No safety net."

The clock struck six as Philippe and Celine took seats in the front row of the lecture hall. A representative from the Chicago Immigrant Advocacy Network stood at the podium, adjusting the microphone as her nervous fingers smoothed out the creases in her "Future Citizen" T-shirt.

"I came to this country seven years ago," she began, her voice steady despite the flutter in her chest. The crowd quieted, turning toward her. "I left Somalia because I believed in the American dream, the idea that if you work hard, follow the rules, and contribute, this country will welcome you as one of its own."

A gentle murmur of agreement spread through the crowd. An older man wearing a veteran's cap nodded gravely. A young couple holding hands, one in a hijab, the other in a "Black Lives Matter" shirt, leaned in to listen.

The speaker took a deep breath. "But becoming a citizen isn't simple. It's a journey, one with many paths." She reached into her bag and pulled out a thick booklet, its pages worn from study. "Right now, I'm preparing for my naturalization test. But for those who don't know, let me explain how this works."

She held up a finger. "First, family sponsorship." A young girl translating for her grandmother perked up. "If you have a relative who's already a U.S. citizen or permanent resident, they can petition for you. Parents, spouses, even siblings, but the wait can take years, even decades, depending on the country."

Another finger. "Second, employment." She pointed to a group of nurses in scrubs near the stage. "Doctors, engineers, professors, if you have skills this country needs, you might qualify for a work visa. But the system is competitive, and corporations often exploit temporary workers."

A third finger. "Third, refugees and asylum seekers." Her voice softened as she looked at a Syrian family sitting nearby. "If you're fleeing war or persecution, America promises safety. But the process is grueling, and too many are turned away at the border."

She flipped through her booklet. "Then there's the Diversity Visa Lottery, 55,000 green cards given out randomly each year to countries with low immigration rates. My cousin won his spot that way." A few chuckles came from the crowd.

"And finally," she said, tapping the cover of her study guide, "once you're a permanent resident, after five years, or three if married to a citizen, you can apply for naturalization. You take the test, swear the oath, and finally, finally, you belong."

In the front row, an elderly Black woman wiped away tears from her eyes.

"But here's the truth," the speaker continued, her tone firming. "These doors exist, but they're heavy. Some are half-shut. Some have invisible locks." She held up her booklet again. "That's why I study every night. Why I practice the civics questions until my voice is hoarse: 'What did the Emancipation Proclamation do?' 'Name one right reserved for states.'"

She smiled then, despite the weight of her words. "Because citizenship isn't just about passing a test. It's about claiming your place in this country's story, one that today reminds us freedom is never finished."

The late afternoon sun slanted through the oak trees, casting shadows on the sidewalk as Celine led her friends and visitors through the neighborhood after the lecture. The air carried the mixed scents of fried plantains, exhaust fumes, and the faint smell of Lake Michigan not far away. Beside her, Uncle Pierre gestured broadly as he spoke, his deep voice rising above the hum of passing traffic.

"Over there," he said, pointing to a squat brick building with a neon Haitian flag taped in the window, "is where most folks send money back home. You'll see the line around the block on Fridays."

Amina, with her sunglasses resting on her head, tilted her chin. "Is it hard? Sending support when you're so far away?"

Uncle Pierre exhaled, rubbing his temple. "Hard? Yes. But what choice is there? When the phone rings and it's your sister saying the roof blew off in the storm, " He stopped himself, shaking his head.

Paulette, the only African American in the group, who had been quiet and watching the street intently, finally spoke. "Englewood's got its own rules. Most of the people in my neighborhood don't have family they've left behind, but sometimes the city tries to break you anyway." She crossed her arms. "The difference is, we get arrested for walking down the wrong block. They only wish they could deport us."

Rosita, with her hands in her jacket pockets, frowned. "My grandmother prays every night that ICE doesn't knock. Ten years waiting for papers. Ten years holding her breath."

Celine, who had been listening quietly, cleared her throat. "And yet, we all keep going." Celine smiled faintly. "What else is there to do?"

Just then, the door of the nearby bakery swung open, releasing the warm aroma of butter and sugar. A round-faced woman in an apron waved. "Pierre! Where have you been hiding?"

Uncle Pierre's serious face broke into a grin. "Ah, Madame Baptiste! Just showing these young folks how we survive."

The woman laughed, wiping her flour-dusted hands on her apron. "Survive? Child, we live. Now come taste this bread before I sell it all."

As they packed into the small bakery, the heaviness of the conversation eased, just a little. The smell of fresh bread, the clatter of trays, and the soft hum of Creole chatter reminded them that isolation wasn't the whole story.

Two days after the lecture, Uncle Pierre took Philippe on a tour of the Haitian Community Center. A bulletin board near the entrance was covered with flyers, some written in clear English, others in hastily translated Creole, advertising everything from free GED classes to emergency legal clinics.

"This is where it all happens," Pierre said, pride warming his voice.

The space buzzed with activity. In one corner, a group of older men hunched over a chessboard; their laughter punctuated the steady click of pieces being moved.

Nearby, a young mother rocked a sleeping baby while filling out paperwork at a folding table, her brow furrowed in concentration.

The walls were lined with framed photos, black-and-white images of early Haitian immigrants in stiff suits and Sunday dresses, alongside lively snapshots of recent cultural festivals, with the bright blues and reds of the Haitian flag draped over proud shoulders.

Pierre led Philippe past a small kitchenette, where a volunteer ladled steaming soup into foam cups for a line of tired-looking day laborers. "We feed anyone who walks in," he explained. "No questions asked." The rich aroma of garlic, thyme, and simmering broth made their stomachs growl.

Down the hall, a classroom was filled with adults bent over workbooks, their pencils scratching as a tutor wrote math problems on a whiteboard. "English and citizenship classes," Pierre whispered. "Some of these folks have been here twenty years and still get tripped up by the test." His voice softened. "But they keep trying."

At the back of the building, a makeshift legal office was filled with file boxes and a hurried-looking woman typing quickly on an old computer. "That's Marjorie," Pierre said. "She helps people apply for asylum, DACA, you know, the Deferred Action for Childhood Arrivals program, whatever they need. Last month, she prevented a family from being deported." His jaw tightened briefly before he shook it off.

As they headed back toward the entrance, Pierre paused by a faded mural of Haiti's mountains and coastline, its colors dulled by years of sunlight. "This place isn't just about survival," he said, running a hand over the peeling paint. "It's about remembering where we came from, and fighting for where we're going." The center radiated warmth, resilience, and the quiet resolve of a community determined not to be forgotten.

The late afternoon sun streamed through the stained-glass windows of the New Covenant Nondenominational Church, casting shards of broken light across the worn wooden pews. Several years ago, Pastor Eli arranged to buy the building from the Catholic Archdiocese, which was consolidating its parishes. The air smelled of candle wax and incense.

Philippe's knee jittered anxiously, his dreadlocks catching the window's light, which twirled around the graying streaks in his hair, glowing like a halo. He looked at Celine sitting beside him. Tonight, they were supposed to learn about the inner workings of the church's justice ministry.

Pastor Eli's voice cut through the murmuring of voices and rustling papers. "Sisters and brothers, we are called to be more than just a house of prayer; we are called to be a house of action."

The retired teacher in the front row, Mrs. Alvarez, nodded so enthusiastically her glasses slipped down her nose. The young lawyer, Mark, from the pro bono clinic, uncapped his pen with a decisive click.

Philippe leaned in toward Celine, his whisper warm against her ear. "Ready for the whole truth?" The scent of his soap cut through the church's mustiness.

Celine smirked. "Raring to go!"

Their fingers brushed as they both reached for the attendance sheet someone had passed around. Philippe didn't pull away, and she didn't either. The stained glass darkened as clouds moved across the sky outside.

"You know," he said, tapping the spreadsheet, "this fight never ends."

Celine looked at her hands and thought about her recent visa problem. She grabbed her notebook, fingered her pen, and got ready to learn from the experts.

At the front of the church, Pastor Eli pointed to a folding table where two volunteers sat alongside a pro bono immigration attorney; their laptops were open, and stacks of forms were neatly arranged. "We've established monthly legal clinics," he explained clearly. "If you're undocumented, if your papers are in limbo, come. Let us walk with you."

Celine sat at the same table just last week, across from Miriam, the soft-spoken attorney who patiently laid out her options like a lifeline. "You're not alone in this," Miriam told her. "We'll stand by you in your documentation case. We fight these cases every day."

Mr. Johnson, a retired steelworker with hands like weathered oak, slid into the pew beside Celine. "My wife and I signed up for the accompaniment program," he said, his voice low and gravelly. "If you need someone with you at court, at a lawyer's office, just say the word."

Celine swallowed hard. The kindness of it, strangers willing to stand beside each other, to serve as a buffer against the cold machinery of the system, tightened something in her chest.

Philippe leaned toward her and whispered, "We've got a good support team."

She nodded, looking around the room. "Yeah," she said softly. "It appears so."

Outside, the wind rattled the basement windows, but inside, the warmth of shared purpose remained steady. And when Philippe's hand brushed Celine's again, neither of them pulled away.

###

Deacon Martha, her silver hair pulled into a no-nonsense bun, flipped open the weathered ledger with a decisive snap. "We've set aside emergency funds," she announced, her voice easily carrying through the quiet room. "For legal fees, for rent if work dries up, no red tape, no shame."

A murmur of approval rippled through the congregation as chairs creaked and everyone shifted in their seats. Celine felt the weight in her chest lift slightly. She thought about the rising costs: the $1,225 filing fee for adjustment of status, the $85 biometrics fee, and how her stomach always sank every time she passed a check-cashing store with its predatory notary fees posted in the window. She could see Philippe doing the same mental math, his journalist's mind automatically turning those numbers into stories: $1,225 equals six weeks of groceries for the Rodriguez family. $85 could pay for a month of someone's diabetes medication.

Deacon Martha adjusted her cat-eye glasses, the gold frames catching the light. "Now don't go thinking this is charity," she said sternly, though her eyes held kindness. "This is what family does. We help when the roof leaks. We bring soup when someone's sick."

Celine remembered the elderly couple who had handed her an envelope last month. "For your nursing books, child," they said, and she thought about how the dishwasher at the hospital cafeteria always saved her the least-bruised fruit. For the first time in months, the tension between her shoulder blades started to loosen.

Philippe leaned in, his warm breath against her ear. "I think I'll add this information to the resource guide," he murmured, tapping the immigration manual he had been working on.

Celine nodded, her fingers brushing his as they both reached for the same page. His hands remained steady, even when hers trembled. Across the room, Pastor Eli saw their silent exchange and smiled, recalling his own youthful love formed during the civil rights marches of another era.

Later that evening, the light slanted through the tall windows, catching dust motes that floated like tiny, suspended stars. Celine sat shoulder-to-shoulder with Philippe on a creaking pew.

Pastor Eli's voice, usually booming from the pulpit, softened as he gently smoothed the well-worn pages of his Bible. Tonight, our Bible lesson will focus on the Exodus story, not as ancient history, but as today's news." His thick fingers traced the verses like a man following a map, while the muffled sound of rainwater flowing through the old pipes filled the background.

Celine's tension lessened. She knew every beat of this story, the crack of whips on Hebrew enslaved people's backs, the Nile turning to blood, Moses' sandals scuffing palace tiles as he demanded, "Let my people go." Now, the words crawled under her skin. The ache in them was familiar, the same one she carried in her ribs every time she checked her visa expiration date, every time she coached a diabetic patient through insulin rationing because they feared clinic paperwork.

Philippe's hand reached for hers. His palm was warm and rough from scribbling notes. He didn't look at her, but his thumb brushed the ridge of her knuckles, once, twice, a silent "I'm here." The contact was electric and comforting. She could smell the starch of his shirt and hear how his breathing hitched when Pastor Eli read Pharaoh's refusal: 'Who is this Lord that I should obey him?'

When they reached the part about the plague of darkness, Celine's pulse quickened. She thought of detention cells with no windows, of clients whispering about icebox rooms where lights stayed on for days. Philippe squeezed her hand tighter, his jaw clenched. She knew what he was remembering: the father they'd accompanied to court last week, deported before his toddler's asthma medication could be refilled.

"The Lord set a pillar of fire to guide them by night," Pastor Eli read, his voice growing stronger.

When the lesson ended, one of the young girls started humming a hymn from her homeland. The melody wavered at first, then became steadier. One by one, others joined in. No one knew all the words, but the sound filled the church like tendrils of hope curling upward.

Outside, a police siren wailed several blocks away. Inside, Celine realized, with a clarity that burned like Moses' bush that was never consumed, that holy ground wasn't a place. It was this: neighbors loving neighbors, hands clasped in the dim light, voices rising imperfectly, the relentless choosing of each other, again and again.

Pastor Eli's voice deepened to a growl, "One last announcement before the benediction. Next week, we march." He flicked a bright orange flyer into the air. The Justice-For-All Rally. Federal Plaza. At noon. We're going to march for Celine. The headline flashed across the top in bold block letters that reminded Philippe of protest signs he'd carried in past campaigns. The paper crinkled as it was passed from hand to hand, smelling faintly of the church's copy machine.

Celine's stomach churned as she saw her story summarized in bullet points: "Nurse. Student Visa Delays. And 437 Days in Processing." The numbers stared back, each digit representing a shift she'd worked double, a used textbook she'd bought, a night staring at the ceiling, questioning if graduation would come before deportation. Philippe squeezed her elbow more tightly than before, steadying her like an anchor.

The young lawyer, Mark, with his tie often loosened, raised his hand as if they were in a courtroom. "I've drafted a petition to expedite Celine's case." His pen tapped against a legal pad, leaving tiny blue ink splashes. "We'll deliver it to the official's office with a delegation, clergy in collars, activists, and families affected. Media's already confirmed."

Celine's pulse pounded in her throat. She had spent months keeping her head down, disguising her accent during clinicals, folding her paperwork into neat, invisible squares in her pocket. Now her name would be called out by strangers in a public square. The thought brought both terror and exhilaration rushing up her spine.

"The *Chicago Tribune*'s sending their justice reporter," Phillip murmured, his breath warm against her temple. "Same one who covered my ICE detention center exposé." Philippe's fingers intertwined with hers on the pew. His touch was feather-light. She squeezed back, once, twice, their silent Morse code flowing through the chaos. "Be brave. You've got this," he reassured her.

Across the room, Deacon Martha was already stacking bulletins into neat piles, her pearl earrings catching the light as she nodded. "I'll bring the good bullhorn," she announced, as casually as if she were saying she'd bring deviled eggs to a potluck.

Outside, an L train rumbled by, shaking the stained glass saints in their leaded frames. But inside, something unshakeable was taking hold. Pastor Eli closed his Bible with a thud that sounded like a gavel. "They'll hear us coming," he promised as he told the congregation to go in peace.

Sister Maria approached Celine as she was leaving the meeting. "If it comes to it," she said softly, "this church will become a sanctuary. No one will be taken from our care without a fight."

Celine's hands trembled at her sides. She had spent months carefully navigating bureaucratic minefields; now, these people were declaring war on her behalf. Grateful tears blurred her eyes, transforming the room into a shimmering watercolor of resolute faces. Mrs. Alvarez pressed a slip of paper into Celine's damp palm. "My spare room's yours if you need it," the older woman whispered, her hands smelling of flour and lavender sachets she kept in her dresser drawers. The lawyer followed, pressing a sheaf of papers into her other hand, his fingerprints smudged in blue ink along the edges. "Your story changes minds," he said, adjusting his glasses. "But only if you're ready to share it."

The wind nipped at their cheeks as Celine and Philippe stood on the church steps, the setting sun casting a blood-red glow on the brick facade. The loud peal of the church bells resonated through Celine's chest, each toll beating like a heartbeat. Philippe stood beside her. Without thinking, she reached for his hand, his fingers instantly closed around hers, their callouses brushing against her skin.

Somewhere downtown, immigration judges were stamping denials; detention centers were locking their doors for the night, but here, on this sacred ground, the bells kept ringing.

Philippe leaned in closer. "They really would hide you in the confessional booth if it came to that," he murmured, nodding toward Sister Maria, who was packing protest signs into her rusty Subaru.

Celine laughed, the sound surprising even herself. The weight on her chest, this constant pressure of forms, deadlines, and fear, lifted just enough to let her breathe. She wasn't just a case number in some government database. She was the nurse who'd held dying Haitian hands in Port-au-Prince. She was the student who aced pathophysiology exams after only three hours of sleep. She was the woman Philippe looked at as if she'd hung the moon, even when her hair was a mess and her scrubs smelled of hospital antiseptic.

As the final bell faded, Celine straightened her shoulders. For the first time since she'd arrived at O'Hare with two suitcases and a student visa, she wasn't just barely getting by.

13

Celine at the Hospital

May 2019

T he fluorescent lights buzzed overhead in the crowded hospital ward, casting a harsh, unflattering glow over rows of iron beds. The air was thick with the sharp scent of antiseptic, layered over the lingering musk of sweat and sickness. Somewhere down the hall, a janitor pushed a mop bucket, the rhythmic squeak of wet rubber against linoleum blending with the low murmur of voices and the occasional groan of pain.

Having won her case, Celine moved through her final clinicals like a woman walking against the wind, steady and deliberate. Her feet ached in her sensible leather shoes, but she refused to slow down. She had learned long ago that stopping meant noticing how tired she was, and noticing meant crumbling.

At the far end of the ward, an elderly Black man named Mr. Dawson coughed into a stained handkerchief, his broad shoulders shaking from the effort. The tuberculosis ward was full, so they placed him here, next to a car crash victim and a young mother recovering from sepsis. Celine adjusted his IV, her fingers briefly resting on his wrist to check his pulse, too fast, too thin.

"Just hang on," she murmured, though she wasn't sure if she was talking to him or herself.

His fevered eyes flickered open. "Nurse, water?" His voice was a dry, raspy whisper, barely audible.

She nodded and reached for the pitcher next to his bed, pouring a careful half-glass. She slipped an arm behind his shoulders, lifting him just enough to drink without choking. He managed a few sips before sinking back against the pillows, exhausted from the effort.

"Thank you," he whispered.

She pressed a cool cloth to his forehead, smoothing back his damp, gray hair.

There was nothing else she could do, not for the TB, nor for the way his breath hitched like a broken engine. Medicine had its limits. But she could sit with him and make sure he wasn't alone.

A commotion near the nurses' station drew her attention, a young intern waving her over, his face tense with panic. Somewhere, a child was crying. Celine took a moment to squeeze Mr. Dawson's hand, then stood, straightening her spine before rushing toward the next crisis.

Her shift wouldn't end for hours. But neither would her resolve.

The next day, Celine moved through the emergency department like a steady stream, her sneakers squeaking against the linoleum as she navigated between gurneys and frantic staff. The air smelled of antiseptic. Somewhere down the hall, a monitor beeped in urgent, irregular pulses. Celine's fingers twitched; she recognized that rhythm. It was the sound of someone slipping away.

A nurse grabbed her arm. "Room 4. GSW to the chest. Family's outside."

Celine nodded, already getting ready. She had seen enough gunshot wounds in Haiti and Chicago to know how this would go. The victim, a young man, barely twenty, lay still under the bright lights, his breathing shallow. The trauma team moved swiftly, shouting orders, but she could see the truth in how the blood pooled too quickly beneath the gauze.

She took a step back. Medicine could only do so much.

Outside the curtain, a woman wailed, high and broken, the mother. Celine took a slow breath before pushing through to where the family huddled, a cluster of trembling hands and tear-streaked faces. The mother's knees buckled when she saw Celine's expression.

"No, no, no, "

Celine caught the woman before she hit the floor, guiding her to a chair. Words wouldn't change anything now, so she didn't try. Instead, she knelt beside her, letting the woman claw at her scrubs, her own throat tightening. The weight of the moment pressed down, another life lost, another family shattered.

But Celine stayed. She had nothing to offer but her presence, her hands steady on theirs when the world spun too fast.

When her sobs turned into hiccups, she stood up. The emergency room still buzzed around her, another ambulance pulling in, another voice calling her name. Celine wiped her palms on her thighs, streaking them with dried blood she hadn't noticed before.

No time to linger or pause. She slowly sipped her cold, bitter, and stale coffee, then moved back into the storm.

Celine moved through the clinic with quiet determination, her hands steady even as exhaustion tugged at the edges of her resolve. The weight of suffering could have hardened her, perhaps should have, by the cruel logic of the world, yet she bore it with remarkable grace. At first light, before the doors opened to the tired and wounded, she knelt by the rusty sink in the back room, lips forming silent prayers that connected her to something beyond the cracks in the linoleum, the shortages in medicine, and the endless wave of human need.

Later, when the woman with the blistered feet flinched at her touch, Celine did not pull away; instead, she let her thumb trace the sign of the cross just above the bandage, a small benediction, unspoken but understood. Faith, for her, was not an abstract fortress; it lived in the press of warm palms against fevered brows, in the extra moment taken to listen when time was the rarest commodity of all. The divine, she had long decided, was not a shield against the world's darkness but the stubborn light by which one can keep seeing it clearly, and love it anyway.

At Bed 6, an elderly Vietnamese man clutched his chest, his face twisted in pain. His grandson, no older than twelve, stood nearby, eyes wide and struggling with broken English: "Grandfather, heart, hurts."

Celine didn't need perfect words to understand fear. She knelt beside the bed, moving slowly and deliberately, and placed her hand on the man's wrist. His pulse fluttered like a trapped bird. She met his eyes and smiled, not a quick, distracted smile of someone rushing to the next crisis, but one that said, "I see you." Then, in careful, measured tones, she said, "You're safe here. We'll help you."

She didn't know Vietnamese, but she understood the language of touch, steady hands, and relaxed eye contact. The man's shoulders eased slightly.

Across the room, a young mother from Guatemala gently rocked her feverish toddler, her lips moving in silent prayer. Celine stopped the nurse's station intern before he hurried past. "Get Marta from housekeeping," she said. "She speaks this woman's language. This mom needs to know we're giving her baby fluids, not just sticking her with needles."

The intern blinked. "How do you even know?"

"Because I listen," Celine said, already turning toward the next bed.

At the far end of the ward, a man in his fifties sat stiffly on a gurney, his work boots hanging loosely, his calloused fingers clutching the edge of the mattress. His chart read, "back pain," but the way he avoided eye contact told Celine more. She picked up the clipboard and scanned the sparse notes: no insurance, no primary care doctor. "Mr. Dawson," she said, sitting beside him. "Are you in too much pain to fill out these forms?"

He hesitated, then ducked his head. "Nurse, I ain't . . . really good at reading."

She didn't miss a beat. "Then let's do it together." She held the clipboard so he could see, her finger tracing each line as she read aloud. His shoulders relaxed. By the time the doctor arrived, he was breathing more easily, not just from the pain relief, but from the relief of being truly seen.

Celine's pager buzzed again. Another patient, another story waiting to be heard. She adjusted her stethoscope and entered the next curtained bay, where a frightened teenager sat clutching his stomach.

"Hey," she said softly. "Tell me what's wrong." And because she made it sound like she had all the time in the world, he did.

The morning sun cast a warm, golden glow over the university campus, reflecting off the brass buttons on Celine's graduation gown as she adjusted her cap in the mirror. The black fabric felt heavy against her skin, with the tassel swaying with each movement, a pendulum marking the end of one chapter and the start of another. She smoothed her hands over the front, her fingers brushing the embroidered letters of her nursing program one last time.

She had achieved it. The conflicts had been resolved. The rest was up to her.

The air outside buzzed with excitement, laughter, camera shutters clicking, and the rustling of programs as families took their seats in the rows of folding chairs. The scent of freshly cut grass mixed with the faint perfume of roses from bouquets carried proudly. Celine's heart pounded against her chest, a rhythm of joy and disbelief.

Her supporters arrived in full force. Community center members showed up in large numbers. Uncle Pierre sat in the front row, dabbing his eyes with a handkerchief. Next to him, Philippe stood tall in his Sunday best. His dark eyes scanned the crowd until they landed on Celine. A slow, proud smile curled on his lips,

"There she is," he said.

She waved at them, her throat feeling tight.

Then, as the procession began, the sound of organ music filled the air, and Celine kept pace with her classmates. The sea of black gowns moved like a living creature, their tassels bouncing in rhythm. To her left, Rosita squeezed her hand. "We did it," she whispered, her voice thick.

"Yes. We did," Celine echoed.

But even amid the surge of triumph, there was a quiet space inside her, an ache no celebration could fill. "Marcus should have been here." He would have cheered the loudest, whooped when her name was called, and swept her into one of his bear hugs afterward. She could almost hear his voice in her ear: "Look at you, Sis. Top of the world."

Philippe felt it too. As the dean began calling out names, his eyes darted to the empty seat beside Uncle Pierre, the one they had deliberately left open. His chest tightened. Marcus should have been here to see this.

They called her by her name: "Celine Marie Laurent."

The applause erupted as her community supporters cheered louder than anyone else. Uncle Pierre quickly stood up, tears streaming down his face. Philippe whistled sharply and brightly through his teeth.

Celine stepped forward, her legs trembling, and accepted her diploma. The weight of it in her hands symbolized more than just paper, it represented every late-night study session, every tear shed over exams, and every moment she pushed through when giving up would have been easier.

As she turned back toward the crowd, her eyes met Philippe's. In that look, they conveyed everything words couldn't: "Love you. This is just the beginning."

After the ceremony, under the shade of an old oak tree, Celine hugged her classmates, her laughter ringing clear. Paulette pinned her nursing pin to her lapel, and Amina pressed a flower into her hand. Philippe handed her a small box; inside, a silver bracelet was engraved with the date. "So, you never forget," he said.

She slipped it onto her wrist, the metal cool against her skin. Somewhere, she liked to think, Marcus was smiling.

The heavy oak door of the Dean's office was slightly ajar, allowing the distant hum of students chatting in the hallway and the subtle aroma of freshly brewed coffee to drift inside. Celine adjusted her hands on her blazer, the same one she'd worn to job interviews, and knocked softly.

"Come in," Dean Hartman's warm voice called.

The office was bathed in late afternoon sunlight, with golden rays bouncing off framed degrees and black-and-white photos of former graduates. The air carried the scent of polished wood and a hint of lavender from a small diffuser on the bookshelf. Dean Hartman sat behind her desk, her silver-streaked hair pulled back into her usual neat bun, her sharp eyes softened by the smile she wore.

"Celine," she said, gesturing to the chair across from her. "Please, sit."

Celine sat on the edge of the leather seat, her stomach fluttering. She had replayed this moment in her mind a dozen times, was it a final evaluation? A recommendation?

Dean Hartman folded her hands on the desk. "I'll get straight to the point. Your clinical evaluations were excellent. Your professors speak highly of your dedication, and your story, your perseverance, is exactly the kind of character we value in nurses." She paused, her eyes locking onto Celine's. "Westlake Memorial has an opening in its emergency department. I want to recommend you for the position. Full-time. Starting in September."

For a heartbeat, Celine couldn't breathe. The words lingered in the air between them, bright and impossible. "A job. A real, full-time job at Westlake." The same hospital where she'd once shadowed as a student, wide-eyed and eager to prove herself. Her pulse hammered in her ears.

She swallowed. "I don't know what to say."

Dean Hartman chuckled. "A yes would suffice."

Celine chuckled, the sound bubbling up from deep inside her chest. "Yes."

That evening, the air was thick with the scent of blooming jasmine as Celine hurried across campus, her heels clicking on the pavement. She had texted Philippe earlier. "Meet me at the garden bench. I have news to share."

She saw him before he noticed her. He was leaning against the iron railing overlooking the university's rose garden, with the golden sunset casting warm light on his face. His tie was loosened around his neck, and his shirt sleeves were rolled up to his elbows, his usual just-finished-work look. A slow smile crept across her lips.

He turned as she approached, his dark eyes lighting up. "You look like you're about to burst."

"I got it," she blurted out. "The job. Westlake Memorial. Full-time, starting in September."

Philippe's face shifted, his grin wide, hesitant, then completely triumphant. In a quick motion, he closed the distance and pulled her into his arms, spinning her once before setting her back down. The scent of his cologne enveloped her as his hands gently cupped her face.

"Celine," he breathed, pressing his forehead to hers. "I knew they'd take you. I knew it."

She laughed, her fingers curling into his shirt. "You had more faith than I did."

"Always." His thumb brushed her cheek, softening his expression. "You're going to be incredible."

The weight of the moment bore down on them. This was it, the start of everything they had been working tirelessly for. The late-night study sessions, shared coffees, and whispered dreams in the quiet hours after sunset.

And as the sun sank below the horizon, painting the sky with streaks of pink and gold, Celine allowed herself to believe, in the job, in the future, in them. For the first time in a long while, everything felt just right.

The night air outside Uncle Pierre's apartment was thick with the smell of grilled meat. Celine leaned against the fire escape, her elbows resting on the rusted railing that was still warm from the day's heat. Below, the city pulsed, cars honked, teenagers laughed on the sidewalk, and somewhere, a radio played lively music, with the bass faintly thumping through open windows.

She felt more than heard Philippe step behind her. He didn't speak; he just leaned against the railing beside her, and the silence felt comfortable in a way only family can create. After a moment, he handed her a cold beverage. She accepted it with a small smile.

"You're thinking too loud," he murmured, eyes scanning the distant skyline.

Celine let out a soft laugh. "Just planning."

Philippe didn't push; he knew better. They had spent years understanding each other's silences and unspoken fears. His mere presence was enough.

She took a slow sip, feeling the cool liquid calm her nerves. The truth was, she was thinking about Marcus, whose dreams had suddenly been taken away. About her mother, back in Haiti, cooking under a flickering generator light because the power had gone out again. About Pierre, who had sacrificed so much to come here, only to realize that the battle was never over.

And yet.

She also reflected on the small victories: how the university had to respond to the protests after the *Tribune* article; the Haitian nurse she met at the detention center rally, who promised to help deliver medical supplies to Tante Rose's clinic in Haiti; and how Deacon Martha slipped extra cash into her bag last week, no questions asked, because she knew she'd send it where it was needed.

The wind picked up, carrying the smell of an approaching storm. Celine closed her eyes, letting it wash over her. She didn't have all the answers. She wasn't exactly sure what lay ahead. She didn't know how to fix a country falling apart with violence and corruption or how to protect the people she loved from a system meant to break them.

But she knew this: she would keep going. Somewhere in the distance, thunder rumbled.

Philippe nudged her shoulder. "Storm's coming."

Celine smiled, a small, tired but genuine smile. "Yeah," she said. "But so are we."

And when the rain finally started to fall, warm and heavy in the Chicago night, she didn't move to go inside. She stood there, face tilted up, and let it wash over her. Because storms had come before, and she was still here.

###

By 2019, the Haitian community in Chicago had moved through their days like figures in a fading photograph, their edges blurring under the weight of impending erasure. The notices arrived in crisp government envelopes, their contents sterile and final: "Your designation under TPS will terminate on July 22, 2019." For Donavan Augustin, it meant the taxi he'd driven for fifteen years, the one with the rosary hanging from the rearview mirror and the worn leather seats polished smooth by countless fares, could become someone else's livelihood by summer's end. He kept the letter folded in his glove compartment, as if the act of hiding it might undo its truth.

In the back corner of a Haitian restaurant in Rogers Park, men hunched over immigration forms, their faces lit by the glow of laptops. The air was thick with urgency. They spoke softly about affidavits, proof of hardship, and how impossible it was to return to a Port-au-Prince where gangs now roamed the streets like unofficial mayors. Some had left Haiti as children; their Creole was hesitant, their memories of the island only fragments, a grandmother's lace curtains, the taste of mangoes stolen from a neighbor's tree.

Celine, working night shifts in the ICU, observed the effects on her community's bodies. Elderly Haitians arrived with advanced cancers, their treatments delayed by fear that hospital records might lead to deportation. Mothers brought children in for asthma attacks but refused paperwork for subsidized inhalers. The clinic where she volunteered on weekends became a place of quiet confessions: "My husband was picked up at the bakery. They didn't let him put on his coat."

The city around them thrived, construction cranes arched over downtown, the mayor praised Chicago as a sanctuary, but in the apartments above Howard Street, families kept suitcases packed. Teens memorized their parents' Alien numbers like incantations. At block parties, the music still played, but the dancing had a desperate quality, as if each song might be the last before the knock came.

When Philippe met Celine at a community meeting that winter, they recognized the same tension in each other: the cautious way of moving through the world, the habit of scanning rooms for exits. He told her about the deportation flight his cousin had been forced onto, how immigration officers had confiscated the man's shoes before boarding, how he'd arrived in Port-au-Prince barefoot and disoriented, his Chicago life reduced to the clothes on his back. She described the elderly patient who'd ripped out his own IV and fled the hospital upon hearing ICE was checking records.

14

Pandemic and Precarity

2020-2024

The last day of normalcy was March 13, 2020. Celine, with her freshly earned RN, stood frozen in the break room of Westlake Memorial Hospital's COVID ICU as the hospital administrator announced visitor restrictions. Around her, experienced nurses exchanged knowing glances, they'd weathered H1N1 and Ebola scares. But their tired silence frightened her more than any pandemic briefing.

"They're talking about using that health law to send people back," Celine said quietly, tapping a news headline about Title 42, enacted on March 20, 2020, by the U.S. Centers for Disease Control and Prevention (CDC) under the Trump administration. It was a public health order that allowed the U.S. government to rapidly expel migrants, including asylum seekers, at the borders under the pretext of preventing the spread of COVID-19.

The Haitian nurses' group chat exploded with voice notes and quick Creole guesses about travel bans. Celine's student visa had just changed to work authorization, what if hospitals laid off foreign workers first? She rinsed the same N95 mask under boiling water while her cousin in Port-au-Prince sent warnings over WhatsApp about deportations.

By April, the morgue trucks had become as routine as the sunset. Celine walked past them every morning at 6:45 a.m. and again at 7:30 p.m., their humming generators the only farewell for the dead. The refrigerated trailers had quietly appeared one night, like uninvited guests

at the hospital's back entrance, and by the third week, she stopped noticing them altogether.

Inside, the hours blurred together during twelve-hour shifts. The
COVID ICU had expanded to occupy two full floors, each room a bleak
mirror of the last, beeping monitors, the steady whoosh of ventilators, the
muffled cries of patients begging for air. Her hands shook from caffeine
and exhaustion as she adjusted IV lines, the chafing from her N95 mask
leaving angry red marks on her cheeks. Sometimes, during rare moments
of stillness, she would lean against the med cart and realize she couldn't
remember the last time she had taken a full breath without the tight elas-
tic pressing against her face.

For months, the nurses worked through their shifts in silence, weav-
ing grief into the rhythm of IV drips and ventilator alarms. Then the vac-
cine rollout came with drive-throughs for the North Shore, but only empty
promises accompanied patients in her hospital. Celine spent her free time
translating flyers into Creole, urging elders to ignore WhatsApp rumors
that the shots meant deportation.

She barely registered the nightly applause for healthcare workers
anymore. When the 7 p.m. cheers drifted through her apartment window, she was usually slumped on her couch, still in her scrubs, peeling
off compression socks as the TV flickered quietly in the background. The
neighborhood's gratitude felt distant, surreal, like something happening
to another person in another life.

The one thing that still pierced the numbness was Mr. Augustin. She'd
recognized him immediately when they wheeled him in. Her neighbor
from 3B, the one who always held the elevator for her after her night shift.
Now he was curled on his side, gasping into a mask, his taxi driver jacket
folded neatly on the chair beside him. When she spoke to him in Creole, his
panicked eyes softened with recognition.

"You'll be okay," she said, even though they both knew it wasn't true.
She stayed past her shift to watch them intubate him. The hiss of the ventilator sealing his fate sounded like a door closing.

Outside, the city teetered between crisis and cautious hope, but in the
dark of her bedroom, the pandemic had no arc, no narrative. There was
only the work. And then, if she was lucky, silence.

Meanwhile, people died in the gaps between policies, their losses
shown in empty church pews, unfunded GoFundMe pages, and entire
rows of seats vacant at the barbershop where men once debated politics

over dominoes. Haitian nurses worked double shifts in COVID units while their elderly parents waited for test results that arrived too late. Taxi drivers disinfected backseats between fares, breathing through makeshift masks as passengers coughed behind plexiglass barriers. Families crowded into studio apartments, rationing hand sanitizer like wartime supplies, the scent of bleach soaking into their skin along with the lingering fear that hospitals meant deportation, not care.

When the morgue trucks finally pulled away from hospital loading docks, they left behind a silence heavier than the bodies they had carried. Survivors moved through the world like burnt trees after a fire, still standing, but hollowed out. The city's reopening pushed forward, shining with promises of resilience, while laundromats and neighborhood storefronts kept their windows covered with memorial notices.

For Celine and her community, COVID was more than just a health crisis. It was a test of survival, solidarity, and the harsh contradictions of American promises. When the first lockdowns began, frontline jobs became both essential and undervalued. No hazard pay, no real safety measures, just masks handed out like afterthoughts and the constant fear of bringing death home to multi-generational households.

Meanwhile, Title 42 quietly unraveled. Relatives who had escaped Haiti's political chaos, only to wait years in Mexico for asylum, were now being deported at the border using pandemic justifications. Celine's childhood friend, Jean, was among them, sent back to Port-au-Prince just as gangs seized control of entire neighborhoods. Phone calls home became a catalog of terror: "They're burning houses. There's no food. The police won't come."

For those already in Chicago, Temporary Protected Status was a fragile lifeline. When Trump tried to revoke it in late 2020, panic swept through the community. Deacon Martha from the church suddenly faced the threat of being separated from her U.S. community. Lawyers rushed to respond. Protests erupted outside Federal Plaza. The courts temporarily blocked the termination, but the damage had already been done.

By 2021, the disparities became impossible to ignore. While wealthier Chicagoans received vaccines at United Center drive-throughs, Haitian elders in West Rogers Park struggled to book appointments online.

Misinformation spread through WhatsApp groups, some fearing deportation if they sought care, others distrusting a government that had previously betrayed them. Community leaders organized Creole-language town halls, but the toll was already clear: candlelit memorials in parking lots for community members lost to the disease.

Then, shocking images of U.S. Border Patrol agents on horseback surfaced, showing them using aggressive tactics to block and confront Haitian migrants near the Del Rio International Bridge in Texas on September 19, 2021. The incident, captured by journalists and shared widely on social media, quickly sparked national and international outrage. For Celine's friends, it wasn't just news; it was a mirror. "That could've been us," someone said at a church vigil. The irony was evident: Haitians in Chicago were saving lives as nurses and EMTs, while Haitians at the border were seen as threats.

When Illinois lifted its final COVID restrictions in 2022, the Haitian community's recovery unfolded at two different paces. Storefront churches reopened with pews only partly filled, older women still wearing masks, while teenagers stayed home and scrolled through sermons on their phones. The owner of JJ's Fresh Market stopped requiring masks but kept the plexiglass divider at the register, cleaning it twice daily as a routine.

For taxi drivers idling outside O'Hare, business picked up again, but trust remained absent. They rolled down windows even in winter, their cabs filled with the scent of bleach and air freshener, worried whenever passengers coughed. At block parties, DJs turned their music back on, but dances fell apart whenever someone sneezed, the crowd scattering like birds before regrouping in awkward laughter.

The pandemic's official end in 2023 brought little change. Celine's church still kept a list of members who had died from COVID. And through it all, the unanswered question remained: When the next disaster comes, a hurricane, a coup, or another virus, will America see Haitians as people to protect or problems to remove? In Chicago's Haitian community, they already knew the answer. So, they kept their bags packed, their papers up to date, and their prayers ready, just in case.

At the annual Haitian Flag Day festival in May 2023, the drums continued to play. Masked dancers moved to the rhythm of lively music, and plates of traditional food were shared with care and respect. But when the speeches turned to politics, anger surfaced. "Biden extended TPS, but he's still deporting people!" a young activist shouted. Celine nodded silently, relief and betrayal, woven together like old Christmas lights.

###

By the end of 2023, the only visible memorial to the heroism of health-care workers during the pandemic was the fading mural on Howard Street, titled "We Won't Forget," which was painted above the faces of nurses and drivers. But the memorial cookouts dwindled each month. People said they were tired of grief. In truth, they were tired of counting.

The virus took more than lives. It stole the way older men used to gather at Original Soul Vegetarian, debating politics over fried plantains. The way mothers would crowd the daycare steps, trading gossip in a fluid mix of Creole, French, and English. The pandemic's end left behind a neighborhood that functioned but hadn't yet healed, its resilience measured by what people no longer dared to do. At night, behind locked doors, some still wiped down groceries, just in case.

When her green card was approved in 2023, Celine framed it next to her nursing license. On her balcony, she finally removed the weather-stripping that had sealed her windows since 2020. The lake breeze carried the distant pulse of a street market carnival, proof that the Haitian community still thrived, even if more faintly. She exhaled for what felt like the first time in three years, her stethoscope heavy around her neck like a priest's stole.

Meanwhile, the winds of political change were sweeping across the nation. Debates over immigration, national security, and America's role as a sanctuary for the oppressed grew more intense. But amid the chaos, one group unexpectedly attracted attention: Haitian immigrants. At the southern border, a large number of Haitians, many of whom initially fled to Brazil and Chile after the earthquake, now traveled thousands of miles north, through jungles and across rivers, hoping for asylum in the U.S. Their sudden visibility increased pressure, reinforcing the idea that enforcement was failing.

Enter Donald Trump, the Republican nominee, whose 2024 campaign focused on strengthening America's borders. To him and his supporters, Haitian immigrants became a symbol, not just of unchecked migration, but of a broader systemic failure. The narrative took hold: they were economic burdens, strains on welfare, and potential security risks. Never mind that studies have shown Haitian immigrants have contributed to the economy

WITNESS IN THE DUST

or that many have built lives, paid taxes, and raised families in the U.S. The rhetoric remained steadfast, reinforcing a larger message of America First.

By mid-2024, everything was in place. A change was coming that would soon alter policies, disrupt lives, and test the country's morals. The signs were clear to those paying attention: the campaign's harsh rhetoric wasn't just empty words. The future for Haitian immigrants in America was uncertain, and significant, rapid changes were on the horizon.

The first warm breaths of early spring had coaxed Chicago back to life. The city's pulse, once muted, fear-laced, now drummed again in bustling farmers' markets, in the raucous laughter spilling from patios, in the tentative but joyful hum of street festivals returning block by block.

And there, at the heart of it all, were Philippe and Celine, rediscovering the world with the wide-eyed wonder of tourists.

They interlaced their fingers as they wandered through Andersonville's Midsummer Fest, ducking into vintage shops, sharing a too-sweet funnel cake dusted with powdered sugar. Philippe pointed out the masked street performers, jugglers, fire-eaters, and Celine leaned into his shoulder, unable to stop smiling. After many months of isolation, the noise, the movement, the life of the city felt intoxicating.

In Lincoln Park, they sprawled on a blanket with takeout from a Haitian food truck, the heavy scents of griot and pikliz reminding them of home, a home they, as their relatives' phone calls reminded them, still reeled from political unrest and violence. The contrast was jarring; as they basked in the luxury of safety, their families in Port-au-Prince whispered warnings about kidnappings, fuel shortages, and protests.

But here, in this moment, beneath the dappled sunlight filtering through new leaves, they chose to focus on what they had, each other.

The pandemic had revealed them to one another in ways they never expected. Celine had seen Philippe's quiet strength as he delivered groceries to elderly neighbors too afraid to leave their apartments. Philippe had marveled at Celine's resilience, the way her hands never faltered even as she intubated patient after patient, always steady, always fighting. They had survived the worst of the storm, and in the fragile peace that followed, they realized they wanted to keep surviving, together.

Their wedding wasn't extravagant. It couldn't be, not after the financial hits of the pandemic. But it was theirs, simple, unpretentious, just a quick ceremony at City Hall, witnessed by a few close friends. Yet, what the legal part lacked in grandeur, they made up for in joy.

The community center they rented for their reception was crowded, laughter and music shaking the walls, the air heavy with the spices of Haitian food. Aunts and uncles who had spent three years in lonely fear now danced freely. Friends who had lost jobs and loved ones let loose in celebration, clapping along as Philippe spun Celine under his arm, her white dress swirling like a promise.

For one night, the burden of the past few years lifted. The future still held uncertainties, Haiti's unrest, the threat of another variant, and the scars they all still bore. But as they raised their glasses in a toast, surrounded by love and music, it didn't matter.

They had made it. They were alive. And that was more than enough, for now.

PART IV

Home Away from Home

15

A Gathering of Truths

July 2024

The American flag hung limp in the hot July air outside the New Covenant Church, its stripes rippling as passing cars stirred the breeze. The marquee outside the church read: "Freedom Service. All Welcome." Inside the sanctuary, ceiling fans circulated the scent of polished pine pews, smoked pork ribs, and simmering collard greens from the fellowship hall kitchen, where the after-service potluck was waiting. It was the Fourth of July, and half the city was dressed in red, white, and blue, with tiny flags in hand.

The church pews weren't empty. Mothers fanned themselves with the day's bulletin, teenagers slouched in the back rows with their arms crossed, lawyers in linen suits sat shoulder-to-shoulder with day laborers who had just clocked out. Some came for the truth. Some came to see what the pastor would dare to say on Independence Day, that sacred American holiday.

A deacon leaned into the pastor's ear, murmuring, "We got more people than Easter, Reverend." But Pastor Eli wasn't smiling. He studied the faces, the undocumented grandmother clutching her purse, the Black millennial who'd started wearing his "I Can't Breathe" shirt again since the election, the Haitian housekeeper who always sat near the aisle. None of them looked like the grinning white families on the supermarket ads flaunting their backyard barbecues. None of them smelled freedom in the charcoal smoke.

Pastor Eli stepped up to the pulpit. "Let the words of my mouth and the meditation of my heart be acceptable," he prayed silently. Then he looked out over the crowd and began to speak. "Today's scripture is from Matthew 24:43: 'I was a stranger and you did not welcome me.' Please pray with me, if you will, on a message entitled Freedom's Fire."

He opened his Bible and continued. "Today we stand under a sky soon to blaze with fireworks, symbols of a freedom declared almost 250 years ago. But freedom declared is not freedom realized. The same nation that lights sparks in the sky also kindles the fires of crisis at its borders, terrifying the refugees, the hungry, and those Scripture calls 'the least of these,' and this contrast invites us to reflect on what true freedom really means."

Pastor Eli wiped sweat from his forehead. "We sing of liberty while detention centers overflow with Haitian mothers, Venezuelan children, Sudanese fathers, and Mexican workers, all fleeing fires we cannot imagine. At least a century ago, people from diverse backgrounds and cultures also sought asylum when this nation was founded. Jesus told us to welcome the immigrant and the stranger, for we are all made in the image of God: the Imago Dei. Together, we are the body of Christ. Yet, in today's America, those desperate to escape persecution are criminalized. Don't you know that when we turn away the migrant, we turn away Christ? When we deny the asylum seeker, we deny the God who delivered the Israelites from Egypt's oppression. Tonight, many of us will gaze in awe at the fireworks. At the same time, let us also consider other fires. The Holy Spirit came as fire, not in the tame sparks of celebration, but a flame that dismantles borders of the heart. Today, as fireworks erupt, let us ask: 'Whose freedom do I celebrate?' Is it just about the past, or the future we're called to build? Let our hearts burn brighter than any pyrotechnic display, until no stranger stands unwelcome, and God's justice lights the fires of freedom in every heart. Amen."

###

Pastor Eli stepped away from the podium and moved toward the crowd. "Brothers and sisters," he started, his voice deep and steady, "we are here today because we have work to do, not just for ourselves, but for those who come after us." He pointed to the teenagers in the room. "These young ones are studying heroes, our heroes. Men like Toussaint L'Ouverture, who fought for freedom when the world said it couldn't be done. Men like

Martin Luther King, Jr., who showed us that justice doesn't come to those who wait, it comes to those who stand up."

A murmur of agreement spread through the room. "But history isn't just in books," Pastor Eli continued. "It's being written right now. Right here. When a boss steals wages because he thinks we won't speak up, that's history. When a landlord tries to evict a family because they don't know their rights, that's history. And every time we teach each other, organize, and demand better? That's how we change it. Some of you may be concerned about getting into trouble. Toussaint caused trouble. King caused trouble. John Lewis got into trouble, good trouble. Trouble is what happens when the world tries to stay the same, and good people refuse to let it."

Pastor Eli exhaled sharply through his nose, more like a sigh than a laugh. He reached for the offering plate, but instead of passing it, he held it high in the air. "This isn't just for donations. It's a reminder: we are called to distribute our gifts. Every soup pot shared, every protest joined, every time we teach the babies that justice has no language." He set the plate down with a clatter. "That's the rent we pay for the space we take up in this world."

Pastor Eli stood before the congregation, his sleeves rolled up and hands outstretched. "I now invite you to the altar," he said. Those seeking prayer, mothers with sons in detention centers, workers who had survived the pandemic, elders who remembered crossing borders in the dead of night, and teenagers holding DACA paperwork formed a circle around him.

The pastor bowed his head.

"God of the Exodus, God of Harriet's midnight journeys, God who breaks chains and flings open prison doors, we come before You today as our ancestors did, in the heat of struggle, in the shadow of empire." His voice was low but carried like embers on the wind.

A woman in the circle wiped her eyes. A young man clenched his fists. The pastor continued, "You heard the cries of the enslaved in Egypt. Hear now the cries of those in cages at the border. You made a way through the Red Sea, make a way now for the Dreamers, the asylum seekers, the ones whose papers are lost in the wilderness of bureaucracy."

The prayer grew more intense and bold. "Just as you raised up Moses, we ask you to raise up lawmakers with courage. You fed the hungry with manna, now feed us with justice, with policies that nourish instead of those that destroy."

A gentle murmur of agreement swept through the group. "And when our feet grow tired, when the night is long, remind us, God, that morning will come. That freedom is still unfolding, like dawn after the darkest hour."

The pastor raised his hands. "Go now, not in despair, but in determination, not in fear, but in fire. The struggle continues, but so does the hope. Amen."

Outside, distant fireworks popped like gunfire.

The humid air clung to Celine's skin as she leaned against the wooden post of the porch, watching the last traces of daylight fade over her neighborhood. Below, children laughed, chasing ice cream trucks down the sidewalk, their joy piercing the quiet of the hot summer evening. But the sound barely registered; her mind was miles and years away.

Her phone buzzed. Another email from the Haitian Alliance Network: "Urgent: DHS Preparing New TPS Terminations." She swiped it away without reading. She already knew the script by heart, the legal challenges, protests, and last-minute reprieves that never quite lifted the weight from her chest.

A burst of laughter came from a nearby rooftop party. Up there, people were drinking, dancing, and enjoying lives free from the threat of immigration limbo. She could almost smell the charcoal from their grill, with the scent of barbecued meat drifting through the open window. Her stomach grumbled from more than just hunger.

Across the alley, the rooftop lights flickered, casting long shadows. Then fireworks exploded in the distance. She didn't look up. Some things, after all, were just noise.

In the late August heat, Uncle Pierre lounged on his back porch, lost in thought. He realized that every Haitian abroad carried a ghost, the spirit of the only nation born from a successful slave revolt. They bore the weight of broken promises by dictators and disasters, the lingering pull of a homeland just beyond their reach. Foreign streets became their new ground, concrete and steel replacing palm-lined boulevards, yet their souls remained anchored to that troubled island in the Caribbean. He kept up with the news stories from across the nation.

In Miami, old men gathered every day around chipped domino tiles, their laughter loud and bright beneath murals of Toussaint and Dessalines. The sound of ivory pieces clacking resembled gunfire, echoing battles left unfinished.

In Montreal, mothers wrapped thick scarves around their children's necks, whispering Creole lullabies softly, songs woven with the heat of a sun they no longer felt. The words floated like smoke in the cold air, a language their kids might someday forget.

In Brooklyn, young professionals typed out wire transfers with stiff fingers, watching half their paychecks disappear into Port-au-Prince's hungry earth. They knew the money would evaporate like rain in cracked soil, but they sent it anyway. Blood had always been thicker than borders.

The world had labeled them victims: earthquake survivors, boat people, TPS statistics. However, those who looked more closely saw the truth.

A boy hunched over a borrowed guitar in a Bedford-Stuyvesant basement, blending kompa rhythms into hip-hop beats, rewriting the soundtrack of his heritage. A professor paused mid-lecture, her voice sharp and clear as she corrected colleagues: "Not the poorest country. The first free Black republic."

These were not victims. They were the newest soldiers in a war that had been raging for two centuries, a fight to reclaim what their ancestors had forged in fire. The world called it resilience, but they knew it by its proper name: freedom's restless, unyielding heartbeat.

16

Heritage of Resilience

August 2024

C eline often reflected on her fluctuating options as an aspiring citizen. Between 2008 and 2024, American immigration policy faced significant challenges, marked by crises, ideological shifts, and evolving public opinion. The country's views on who should receive refuge, who belongs, and who should be turned away have evolved significantly with each administration, sometimes being compassionate, sometimes strict, and sometimes a mix of both.

When Barack Obama took office in 2009, America was still recovering from the Great Recession, with its people cautious of outsiders but compassionate toward humanitarian crises abroad. His administration discussed reform, creating a pathway to citizenship for millions living in the shadows, but Congress, divided by partisanship, refused to act. So, Obama used executive power whenever possible. In 2012, he established DACA, protecting young undocumented immigrants from deportation, a gesture of mercy for those who knew no home but America.

But enforcement also became a key part of his legacy. Deportations rose sharply, driven by programs like Secure Communities, which made local police act as extensions of federal immigration authorities. When the severe earthquake struck Haiti in 2010, Obama granted TPS to its survivors, only to resume deportations a year later, despite cholera and political unrest sweeping the island. Critics called it cruelty; the administration argued it was necessary.

Then came Donald Trump, riding a wave of nativist fury. He promised a wall, mass deportations, and a crackdown on "chain migration." His administration delivered. Travel bans targeted Muslim-majority countries. Families were torn apart at the Mexican-American border, and children were caged in detention centers. And for Haitians, the message was clear: You are not welcome.

Trump referred to Haiti as a "shithole country" during a closed-door meeting, a sentiment that influenced policy decisions. He moved to revoke TPS for nearly 60,000 Haitians, forcing them to choose between exile and living underground. His "Remain in Mexico" policy stranded asylum seekers in dangerous border towns, while expedited removals sent Haitians back to a homeland sinking into gang violence. Although the courts blocked some of his harshest measures, the message was clear: America's doors were closing.

Joe Biden entered the White House promising to restore humanity to immigration policy. He reversed Trump's travel bans, strengthened DACA, and extended TPS for Haitians as their country descended into chaos. However, the border was overwhelmed by a record number of migrants, and political pressure forced his hand. At first, he maintained Trump's Title 42 expulsions, using pandemic-era rules to turn away thousands, including Haitians, who gathered in bleak camps under bridges in Del Rio, Texas. The images caused outrage. Over time, Biden changed his approach: humanitarian parole programs offered legal options for some, even though deportation flights to Haiti continued, landing in a capital controlled by gangs.

Throughout it all, the American people remained divided. Some viewed immigrants as a burden, while others saw them as an essential part of the nation. Cities like Chicago and New York struggled with the influx of new arrivals, while red-state governors bused migrants north as a political spectacle. The courts clashed with the White House, Congress stayed deadlocked, and the world watched as the U.S. oscillated between offering refuge and turning people away.

And Haiti, poor, beleaguered Haiti, became a symbol of America's contradictions. Protected one day, expelled the next. Given shelter, then cast out.

###

On Uncle Pierre's cluttered dining table, stacks of flyers, petitions, and newspaper clippings formed uneven towers. Celine sorted through a folder labeled "Neighborhood Association: Immigration Resources," her fingers pausing on a pamphlet for the upcoming legal clinic.

Pierre set a steaming mug of coffee in front of her, the thick aroma cutting through the musty smell of old paper. "You remember Jean-Luc from the association?" he asked, settling into the chair across from her. "He's organizing another letter-writing campaign to Congress, this time for the temporary protected status extension."

Celine looked up, frowning. "I thought that was resolved last year."

Pierre shook his head, absentmindedly stirring his coffee. "Resolved? No. Maybe delayed. These protections are always temporary in name and in practice. Every few years, we have to prove all over again why our people deserve to stay." He tapped the table for emphasis. "That's why the Haitian Coalition keeps pushing, because if we don't, who will?"

Celine picked up a brochure from the Haitian American Museum, examining the vibrant artwork on the cover. "Did you see the new exhibit?"

"Not yet," Pierre admitted. "But your cousin Frantz volunteered there last weekend. He said half the visitors were parents bringing their children, kids who've never set foot in Haiti but need to understand where they come from."

Celine traced the edge of the brochure. "It's not just about preserving the past. It's about making sure the rest of Chicago sees us. That they remember we're here, that we contribute, that we belong."

Pierre leaned forward, his elbows resting on a spread of meeting minutes. "Exactly. And it's not just the museum. The free legal clinic at St. Damien's, the job training at the community center, the after-school programs, these things matter. Especially now, with so many new families arriving."

Outside, children's laughter floated up from the courtyard, a stark contrast to the seriousness of their conversation. Pierre looked in the direction of the sound before continuing. "That's why I keep telling you. You should join the Haitian health professionals' network." Pierre scolded. "We need people like you, Celine. People who understand both worlds, the medical system and what our community faces."

Celine exhaled slowly, her gaze drifting to the framed photo on the wall, her grandparents' house in Port-au-Prince, its porch lined with rocking chairs that would never hold them again.

Pierre followed her eyes. "You think change happens by accident? It takes effort. Showing up at city council meetings. Meeting with legislators. Making sure our people know their rights when ICE comes knocking." He pushed a newspaper toward her, a headline about recent raids. "Fear keeps people silent. But silence won't protect us."

Celine set down her coffee, which was now lukewarm. "What if it's not enough? What if the laws keep changing against us?"

Pierre's voice softened. "Then we change the laws. Or the people making them." He unfolded a flyer for an upcoming voter registration drive. "Last year, we helped elect the first Haitian-American to the school board. We have a Haitian-American Attorney General. Next year, maybe the state-house. Progress is slow, but it's real."

A car honked outside, drawing Celine's attention to the window. The sun had dipped lower, casting a golden glow on the brick buildings.

"You're right," she said finally, tucking the voter drive flyer into her bag. "I'll talk to the nurses' union about partnering with the legal clinic. And I'll be at the next association meeting."

Pierre smiled as he refilled her mug. The coffee steamed between them, bitter, pungent, and sustaining like the work ahead.

Celine carefully arranged golden-brown portions of crispy fried meat along-side fluffy white rice studded with dark red beans on two familiar chipped plates. Steam rose in wispy curls toward the yellowing fluorescent light.

"You seasoned this just like we did back home," Pierre remarked appreciatively, inhaling deeply as he settled into his usual chair at the worn Formica table. The vinyl seat cushion sighed beneath his weight.

Celine smiled, placing a small bowl of brightly colored pickled vegetables between them. "Mrs. Toussaint spent last Saturday teaching me her exact recipe. She says her granddaughter won't touch it unless the peppers are sliced paper-thin like this." She demonstrated the precise cut with her fingers.

Pierre chuckled, shaking out his faded blue napkin. "These American-born children, they demand the flavors of their heritage but want everything adapted to their modern tastes." His expression grew more serious as he poured both of them glasses of iced tea, the condensation already forming on the mismatched tumblers.

"The school board meeting notices arrived yesterday," he said, nodding towards a stack of papers on the counter. "They've approved our Haitian Heritage curriculum for the freedom-school program, but not without pushback from people who want to cancel our history."

Celine's eyes brightened as she handed Pierre the homemade hot sauce. "I've been working on lesson plans, not just about the food, but about our heritage. The children should understand that their story didn't start when their parents arrived here," she said, tapping the table for emphasis. "Jean Baptiste Point du Sable established his trading post right where the Chicago River meets Lake Michigan in the 1780s. A man from Saint-Domingue, what would become Haiti, founded what would grow into this great city." Celine nodded thoughtfully, carefully slicing into her pork. "Sometimes I stand by that bronze memorial plaque near the riverwalk and try to imagine his first winter here. How different everything must have looked back then."

"Probably not so different from how our parents saw this city when they arrived," Pierre mused between bites. "That same mix of hope and determination, knowing that with enough courage and hard work, a person could build something lasting."

They ate in comfortable silence for a moment, the familiar flavors connecting them across generations. Through the open window floated the sounds of their neighborhood, the squealing brakes of a city bus, snippets of conversations in Creole, Spanish, and English, the distant laughter of children playing jump rope in the courtyard.

Celine's eyes moved to the refrigerator calendar, where the date of the upcoming heritage festival was circled in red. "I'm going to suggest that Mrs. Toussaint take her grandchildren to the festival. I'll share the stories I've gathered. The festival is the perfect place. The stories mean more when they come with the smells and tastes, don't they?"

Pierre smiled approvingly, pushing his empty plate aside with satisfaction. Some traditions, they both understood, were too vital to lose. Whether passed through recipes shared in steaming kitchens, stories told over worn tables, or simple acts of remembrance that connect children to ancestors they might never meet, in a homeland they might never see, but whose legacy lives on in every bite and every carefully preserved memory.

###

The golden light of late summer slanted across the busy festival grounds, catching the edges of Celine's banner as it rippled in the humid breeze: "Our Roots, Our Stories: Preserving Haitian Legacy." Around her, the West African drummers' final notes blended into the joyful chaos of the festival, children shrieking near snow cone stands, elders debating politics in the shade, and the sizzle of plantains from a nearby grill.

Celine adjusted a slightly wilted flyer about TPS renewal clinics, her fingers leaving damp streaks on the paper. Even in the fading August heat, the booth stayed lively. Amina's clothesline display of children's drawings, vivid crayon portraits labeled "My Family's Journey," twirled gently above vintage maps tracking Haitian migration to Chicago and the Evanston suburbs. Rosita leaned across the table, switching smoothly between Spanish and English as she guided a Dominican couple to free legal aid resources.

Then Paulette's elbow brushed against Celine's ribs. "Those guys by the jerk chicken stand," she murmured through a tight smile, nodding toward two men in ill-fitting polo shirts. Their eyes scanned the crowd like they were inventorying livestock, their hands suspiciously free of festival food or flyers. "CBP or ICE. Same thing last year at the Filipino fiesta, they took Tita Maricel's nephew right from the food line."

Celine's stomach clenched. She darted a glance at Pierre, who had frozen mid-sentence in his conversation with Mr. Ndiaye from the Senegalese Association. The older man followed their gaze and immediately understood, shifting his bulk to block the agents' line of sight to the three undocumented teens working at the hibiscus drink booth.

"Keep talking like we're just gossiping," Rosita whispered, pressing a sample of food into a visitor's hand with exaggerated cheer. "But Amina, that 'Know Your Rights' poster needs to face outward now."

Amina casually flipped the display, and the bold red letters suddenly became visible to the passing crowds. Celine's pulse hammered in her ears as the men started moving, not toward them, but toward the Guatemalan textile cooperative's booth where a young mother balanced a baby on her hip.

"Hey!" Paulette barked suddenly, loud enough to turn heads, as she stepped into their line of sight. "You want to try some authentic pikliz?" She bodily inserted herself between the agents and their target, thrusting forward a jar of blistering-hot pepper relish. "Special family recipe, if you can handle it."

The taller man recoiled. For a brief suspended moment, the festival sounds grew muffled: the drum workshop's rhythm, the squeal of a toddler chasing bubbles, as every migrant within earshot recognized the threat. Then Pierre boomed, "Ah! The heroes here are protecting us from dangerous cabbage slaw!" and the crowd burst into laughter. The men stepped back quickly, scowling.

Celine exhaled as the mother stepped back, but her hands still trembled when she turned to the next visitor.

From the main stage, the opening chords of a Haitian band erupted, with brass notes piercing through the thick air. The crowd cheered, rushing toward the music, momentarily blurring the line between spectator and performer. Celine took three deep breaths before rejoining her friends, silent guardians of this fleeting joy.

17

The Great Debate

P hilippe sat at their kitchen table, focused on his computer screen. Celine glanced over at him. He was deep in thought, and she didn't want to disturb him. She turned her attention to the flickering Christmas lights on the tree in their living room. In a reflective mood, her mind refused to be still. For many years, the issue of immigration has divided nations, balancing economic hopefulness with cultural caution, humanitarian goals with security concerns. The debate wasn't just about numbers or policies; it was a clash of perspectives, with each side seeing reality through a different lens.

She had done extensive reading while preparing for her naturalization test, eagerly studying everything on the recommended reading list. However, her curiosity prompted her to explore the arguments on both sides of the issue more deeply. On one side were those who viewed immigration as a key driver of progress. They pointed to history: how newcomers had boosted economies, revitalized aging workforces, and enriched societies with new ideas and traditions. To them, borders were more than just lines on a map; they were gateways to opportunity, for both nations and individuals seeking refuge or a better life. They argued that without immigrants, industries would struggle, innovation would slow down, and society's moral fabric would weaken if the vulnerable were turned away.

Yet where one side saw benefits, the opposition saw risks. They warned about unchecked flows overwhelming public resources, wages being kept down by an oversupply of labor, and communities facing rapid demographic changes. For them, immigration was not just an economic issue but also a matter of sovereignty, identity, and security. Borders, in their view, lay at the heart of national order, and without strong controls, chaos could ensue.

The tension between the two perspectives was hard to reconcile. One side prioritized growth and change, while the other focused on stability and the status quo. One emphasized pluralism, while the other favored assimilation. The disagreement was not only political but also philosophical, a deep split over a nation's primary focus.

Amid this divide, fragile but possible compromises emerged. Some nations tested balanced systems, combining stricter border controls with legal migration pathways, merit-based selection, and humanitarian exceptions. Guest worker programs aimed to meet labor demands without provoking cultural backlash, while regional policies allowed cities and states to tailor their integration efforts to meet local needs. However, no solution satisfied everyone; the most enduring approaches acknowledged that immigration was neither simply a blessing nor a threat, but a complex reality in a nation where almost everyone came from somewhere else. Still, history has shown that societies succeed not by favoring one extreme over the other but by finding a middle ground where economics, security, and humanity can coexist.

The studio lights at the independent TV station buzzed faintly like sleepy wasps, casting a cold glare over the makeshift set. The set was intentionally simple: no flashy graphics, no corporate logos, just a semicircle of chairs illuminated by warm light against a backdrop of a broken American flag, its stripes rearranged into the shapes of human figures walking single file toward the horizon.

The prompter flickered. In the control booth, a frazzled producer named Marissa buried her face in her hands as the master audio feed sputtered to life with a screech of feedback.

"Showtime," she announced.

Overhead, the "On the Air" light blinked red.

At the center of the stage, Philippe adjusted his microphone, his sharp eyes scanning the audience. To his left sat four panelists, each a living proof of America's fractured immigration system.

Philippe leaned in, his voice steady despite the chaos. "Welcome, family," he began, his Haitian accent softening the gravity of his words. "Tonight, we ask: 'Who gets to call Chicago home?' In our discussion of the issues, we want to show how freedom is sometimes withheld based on one's origin. Let's get uncomfortable. Let's get started."

###

María González, a community organizer from Little Village, leaned forward, her voice steady but her knuckles whitening around her notes. "You want historical context? Let's start with the Bracero Program, a form of legal exploitation. My abuelo picked lettuce for pennies while being called a wetback. Then came Operation Wetback, mass deportations disguised as patriotism." She paused as the crowd murmured in recognition.

And don't let them fool you with DACA," her voice cracked. "Yes, it saved 600,000 of us, but why were our Haitian siblings left out?"

A teen sitting in the front row held up a sign: "Obama deported my dad." María pointed at it. "Exactly; 2.5 million deportations under Obama, more than any president. But in 2016?" She scoffed. "Trump made racism official."

###

Jean-Pierre Baptiste, a lawyer who fled Haiti after the earthquake, held up a worn photo of the Krome Detention Center. His usually booming voice was quiet, making the crowd lean in. "1980. Cubans arrived in Miami and got asylum in months. Haitians? Branded 'economic migrants,' locked on ships like slaves." He tapped the photo. "Same story in 2010: TPS was a bandage, not a solution. By 2017, Trump canceled TPS."

A woman in the audience wiped away tears as Jean-Pierre continued speaking. "They whipped Haitians in Del Rio like it was 1823, not 2021. Yet Ukrainians, God bless them, got parole in weeks. What's the difference?" He looked out at the crowd. "Anti-Blackness. Full stop."

###

Linh Nguyễn, a Vietnamese-American professor, adjusted her glasses, her calm demeanor hiding the fury behind her research. "The Chinese

Exclusion Act was the first law to ban a whole race. Not a nationality, a race." She allowed that to hang in the air. "Then came Japanese internment, citizens in camps. Fast-forward to 1965: They let in Asian doctors and engineers to fuel capitalism, then called us 'model minorities' to divide us from Black and Brown movements."

She clicked on a slide showing ICE data: over 15,000 Asian deportations from 2010 to 2020. "My Cambodian students' families built this country after surviving genocide. Now? Trump deported them for parking tickets." Her voice grew louder. "And when COVID hit, they blamed us, while our elders were beaten in the streets."

Sean O'Reilly, the son of Irish immigrants and a former ICE agent turned whistleblower, shifted uncomfortably. "My people were called drunken monkeys in the 1900s. But here's the truth: By the 1960s, we became White." He gestured to Linh. "Unlike her community," he said with a nod toward Lihn, "we weren't banned for our race. Unlike Jean-Pierre, we weren't called 'diseased.' Unlike María, we weren't called 'criminals' for existing."

Then, he dropped a bombshell: "I processed deportations. Saw Haitians jailed for years while Europeans got court dates. The system's rigged, and I helped rig it." The crowd gasped.

Philippe stood and moved toward a whiteboard. "So, here are a few statistics." He pointed to a screen showing deportation statistics.

Haitians: 10,000 deported (2017)

Mexicans: 250,000+ annually

Europeans: Less than 5,000

A young activist shouted, "What do we do?"

Linh grabbed the mic. "Abolish ICE? Yes. But first, recognize the hierarchy. Europeans land on their feet. Asians are 'good' until we're not. Latinx and Haitians? We're in a crisis."

Jean-Pierre added, "Solidarity isn't optional. When they came for Haitians, Black Lives Matter stood with us. Who else will accept the challenge?"

The crowd erupted in cheers. As the panel wrapped up, Philippe whispered to the speakers, "Now the real work begins." The panel discussion was over, but the reckoning had just begun.

###

Of course, there was backlash. An ultraconservative group heard about the panel discussion. The response was swift and intense, quickly spreading across Twitter, Facebook, and other social media platforms. One conservative TV station agreed to host a panel featuring the group as a counter to the liberals' statements.

The conservative panel sat beneath intense studio lights, their faces stiff and eyes filled with conviction. Across the polished oak table, a banner behind them read: "Protect Our Nation, No Compromise." The air hummed with tension. They argued for stricter immigration policies and enforcement measures. Their arguments also suggested a form of superiority.

At the head of the table, Senator Mark Harlow leaned forward, his knuckles pressed against the wood. "Let's be clear," he said, voice low but razor-sharp. "What happened at that leftist liberal panel wasn't a debate, it was an insult." The audience murmured in agreement, a wave of nodding heads passing through the audience. A camera panned across the crowd, men in pressed suits, women clutching notepads, their expressions tense with shared outrage.

Next to Harlow, Dr. Linda Pierce adjusted her glasses, lips pursed. "They talk about 'compassion,' but what about the American worker?" Her fingers tapped impatiently. "Every day, our citizens are passed over for jobs while businesses hire cheap labor from across the border. Wages plummet. Communities suffer. That's not compassion, that's economic sabotage."

To Pierce's right, retired Colonel James Ryker sat upright, his military demeanor firm. "National security isn't negotiable," he barked. "Open borders mean open season for criminals, cartels, and worse." His gaze swept the room, lingering on each face as if daring anyone to dissent. "We have laws for a reason. Ignoring them isn't progress, it's anarchy."

A man in the front row clenched his fists. He had driven from Ohio to express anger that his construction job was awarded to a crew of migrants. He could still hear their foreign chatter and see their knowing smirks.

A woman near the back shifted uncomfortably. She remembered the news reports, gang violence, overdoses, a stabbing in her niece's school district. Stories the liberals dismissed as "fearmongering," but her fear was genuine.

Then came Pastor John Caldwell, his voice a slow, simmering burn. "This isn't just about numbers; it's about the contamination of the soul of this country." He spread his hands, palms up. "Our traditions, our language, our faith, these are the pillars that built America. If we allow our cities to be flooded with people who reject these pillars, what's left?" The crowd murmured again, louder now. A teenage boy in a "Make America Great Again" hat nodded fiercely.

Senator Harlow seized the moment. "And let's talk about the cost," he snapped. "Schools are overcrowded. Hospitals overwhelmed. Welfare drained dry, while our own veterans sleep on the streets!" The audience erupted with angry shouts and scattered applause. A woman near the aisle clutched her purse tighter, thinking about the clinic where she waited three hours last week, surrounded by faces she didn't recognize.

Pierce leaned in. "They call us heartless. Look at our homeless, our addicts, and our abandoned veterans. Charity begins at home."

The energy in the room crackled, a blend of fury and resolve. These weren't just words; they were promises.

An onlooker in the crowd stood up, his jaw clenched. "Enough talk. It's time for action." The crowd roared.

Outside, the city lights blurred against the night sky, indifferent. But inside, beneath the glare of cameras and the weight of conviction, a battle line was drawn.

18

Freedom's Resilience

JANUARY 2025

P romises once hindered by political opposition transformed into action after President Trump took the oath of office for his second term. The administration's already strict immigration policies grew even tougher. The "zero tolerance" policy expanded, detentions increased, asylum laws were tightened, and deportation raids resumed with a level of precision that felt personal. Family separations, which had been condemned, were quietly institutionalized under new legal frameworks. For millions of undocumented residents, including those who had lived in the U.S. for decades, the ground beneath them became unstable.

Cities like Chicago responded quickly by pushing back. Mayors reaffirmed their sanctuary policies, pledging to protect residents from federal overreach, while community organizers prepared for the worst. Lawyers volunteered around the clock to defend against deportation. Churches and nonprofits stocked emergency funds for vulnerable families. However, this defiance only strengthened the administration's resolve. ICE operations became more aggressive, targeting not just criminals but anyone without papers, delivery drivers, grandparents, and students like Marcus who had dared to escape their past.

The nation was split along familiar lines. Some hailed the crackdown for maintaining law and order; others saw it as cruelty hidden behind policy. Tensions grew in the streets, with protests swelling outside detention centers.

Employers concealed their workers, and teachers kept hotline numbers in their desks, ready to call if a child's parent didn't come home.

It was in this America, raw, divided, and bracing for impact, that Pastor Eli took action.

The weight of the situation sometimes kept Pastor Eli awake at night. When systems failed, doors slammed shut, and entire communities were pushed to the margins, a new way of living started to emerge. It didn't ask for permission. It didn't wait for legislation or approval. It simply existed, a living, breathing network of sanctuary and solidarity, stitched together by those who knew all too well the cost of exclusion.

It started with spaces claiming they were safe, not just in theory but in reality. Churches stayed open all night, turning their pews into makeshift beds for families escaping ICE raids. Universities provided scholarships regardless of immigration status. City councils reallocated funds from police budgets to legal defense teams because justice should never depend on the language you speak or the documents you lack.

However, this was more than just providing a refuge; it was also about rebuilding. Housing collectives bought apartment buildings and allocated units for newcomers at affordable prices, no predatory leases, no hidden fees. Labor unions grew their membership by organizing dishwashers and day laborers, demanding wages that didn't force parents to choose between rent and groceries. Hospitals trained staff to recognize the hollow look of trauma and the unspoken wounds of those who had crossed deserts, survived wars, and outrun storms.

And beneath it all, an unseen web hummed with urgency: encrypted chats filled with alerts about checkpoints, a network of volunteer drivers moving people under the cover of night, cash and medicine exchanged hand to hand until they reached borders no official would cross.

The thunderous words of politicians rang hollow in neighborhoods where everyone was from somewhere else. When ICE vans rolled in, they found sidewalks packed with protesters, teachers, nurses, retirees, linking arms in a human barricade, and employers who once fired workers over expired papers now faced strikes. Landlords who tried to exploit found their buildings picketed, and their reputations tarnished.

This brave new world wasn't perfect. There were still evictions, still raids, and moments when fear threatened to wipe out hope completely. But for the first time, the future felt within reach.

The wind rattled the windowpanes of the small apartment where Celine and Philippe had begun to build their life together. The January wind carried howls of winter and an uneasy, tense feeling that had lingered since the election. The warmth inside provided a refuge, not just from the cold but also from the ugliness that had started to seep into their daily lives.

Celine stood by the stove, stirring a pot of pumpkin soup, the warm aroma of nutmeg and thyme wrapping around her like a cozy shawl. The only sound was the rhythmic scraping of the wooden spoon until Philippe's key turned in the lock.

He stepped inside, shoulders tense beneath his coat, his usually bright eyes clouded. The smell of fresh air clung to him as he dropped his satchel by the door, heavy from the day's interviews.

Celine didn't need to ask how his assignment had gone. The tightness in his jaw told her everything. She turned the flame down low and moved across the room, pressing her palms against his chest and feeling the rapid beat of his heart beneath her fingers.

"Tell me," she murmured.

Philippe exhaled, his breath warm on her forehead. "Another ICE raid. Families separated. Kids, Celine, little kids, crying for their parents. And the officers just stood there without expression." His voice cracked. "Like it was routine."

Her fingers clenched his shirt. Flashbacks flooded her mind, faces from her hospital shifts, patients too scared to ask for help, whispered conversations among staff in hallways about who might be in danger.

"We have to do something," she said quietly.

He cupped her face, his thumbs tracing the soft curve of her cheeks. "We are doing something. But it's not enough." His gaze flickered over her, taking in the steadiness in her dark eyes and the quiet strength that had drawn him to her from the beginning. "You exhaust yourself at the hospital, and I chase stories that feel like they disappear into the void. What else can we do?"

She leaned into his touch. "We fight smarter, my dear husband. We watch and take notes. We educate ourselves. We understand our rights. Use what we have." Her mind raced, her medical skills, his platform, their networks. "We find allies. Lawyers, pastors, community leaders, and people who can shield those being targeted. We stand in solidarity. We don't let fear win."

The corner of his mouth lifted. "You say that like it's simple."

"Not simple," she corrected. "Necessary."

He kissed her then, slow, deep, pouring every ounce of gratitude and resolve into it. When they parted, he rested his forehead against hers.

"Okay." His voice was rough but steady. "We build a net. One that our people can't slip through."

The soup was forgotten as they moved to the couch, fingers intertwined, heads bent over Philippe's laptop. Plans formed between them, safe houses, "Know Your Rights" workshops, and underground networks. The world outside grew colder and darker, but here, in the glow of the screen and the warmth of their shared purpose, something fierce and unbreakable took root.

Frigid January air nipped at the ankles of those rushing into the South Side community center, its red-brick facade covered with flyers announcing the teach-in written in bold block letters: "Whose Freedom? Whose Future?" Inside, warmth hummed through old radiators as neighbors stamped snow off their boots.

They arrived in winter coats and work scrubs, in church suits and college hoodies, filling folding chairs until the metal legs groaned. A pensioner with a cane adjusted the framed photo of Dr. King on the podium, his "I Have a Dream" speech reprinted beneath the glass like a sacred text. The date on the flyers, January 16, 2025, stood out with quiet irony. In four days, a new president would take the oath of office, one who'd called their neighborhoods "war zones" and their ancestral homelands "shitholes."

At the back, volunteers hung a banner over cracked plaster: "MLK Didn't Just Dream, He Organized." Teenagers handed out photocopied sheets with hotline numbers for immigration lawyers and rapid-response networks. Near the window, Celine pressed her shoulder against Philippe's.

She still wore her scrubs from the morning shift. Philippe's notebook was already filled with questions.

The room buzzed with a tension unrelated to the weather. Not when ICE raids were taking fathers from bodegas in Albany Park. Not when voting rights were being stripped away in statehouses across the Midwest. Dr. King's words hung unspoken in the air: Freedom is never voluntarily given by the oppressor.

A grandmother in the front row adjusted her glasses, her knuckles as gnarled as cherry roots. She marched at Selma in '65. Next to her, a high school junior held his smartphone, live-tweeting from Standing Rock, a Native American territory straddling the border of North Dakota and South Dakota, and the site of the historic #NoDAPL (Dakota Access Pipeline) protests in 2016–2017. Between them stretched fifty-two years of unfinished revolution.

When the first speaker grabbed the mic, the event organizer, with a voice like a bass drum, the murmurs fell silent. Outside, the wind howled around the building's corners. Inside, something warmer than hope took hold: the relentless, breathing fire of a people who refused to lose their freedom twice.

Bradley stepped up to the microphone, adjusting his glasses as he looked over the audience. He was tall, with dark skin that glowed in the sunlight and a crisp white shirt with sleeves rolled up. The podium wobbled slightly when he leaned on it, but his voice stayed steady. "Good morning," he began, and the murmurs quieted. "We're here today to talk about freedom, what it means, what it costs, and what it demands of us."

This wasn't just a protest or a political rally. It was a teach-in, a celebration of resilience, of cultures merging and enriching each other, and of the simple joy of being together under the same sun.

"Liberty isn't a possession; it's a promise," he declared. Now, standing before an audience of Black faces, White faces, and Brown faces, all watching, all listening, he felt the truth of it.

"So today," he said, "we're not just celebrating Black freedom. We're celebrating the idea that none of us are truly free until all of us are." His hands lifted slightly, palms open, as if offering the words to the crowd.

"Oppression doesn't stop at race. It slithers into labor, into gender, into every corner where power tells people they don't deserve better."

The applause started slowly and then grew louder. Someone whistled. A baby cried out, and its mother gently bounced it, whispering hush against its forehead. Bradley stepped back, allowing the moment to settle. The air already buzzed with something alive, something vital. At this MLK celebration, a day-long teach-in, the past wasn't just a story to be told; it was a spark to be ignited. And the auditorium, the people, and the very ground beneath them all seemed to lean in, listening.

The atmosphere grew thick with anticipation. This was more than a rally; it was a lesson in history, a call to action. Pedro stood at the podium, with a banner that read "No Borders in Humanity" beside him. His deep, steady voice resonated clearly over the crowd.

"Let's talk about walls," he said, gripping the edges of his notes. "Not just the ones made of steel and concrete, but the ones built in minds, in laws, in the stories we tell about who belongs."

The crowd fell silent. An older woman at the front, her face weathered from years of sun and hardship, nodded slowly. A college student in the back stopped texting and put their phone away.

Pedro leaned in. "People act like Mexicans just started crossing the border yesterday. But we've been part of this land long before it had a name. Before the U.S. drew lines through deserts and rivers, our ancestors built towns, raised families, and grew food that fed nations." He paused, letting the weight of that truth settle. "And now? Now they call us invaders for wanting to work, to live, to survive."

Celine, sitting beside Philippe, felt her chest tighten. She realized that her hunger for safety and opportunity was overwhelming. Philippe's hand reached for hers, his fingers intertwining with hers in quiet support.

Pedro held up a newspaper clipping. "They say everyone crossing is a criminal. But the people risking everything, they're mothers. They're kids. They're folks fleeing wars and storms this country helped create." His voice cracked for a moment. "And instead of help, they are given cages, tear gas, and lies."

A murmur of agreement spread, broken by a loud "That's right!" from a man wearing a T-shirt from a construction company.

Pedro wiped his brow as the heat of the day shimmered on his skin. "So, when they talk about walls, remember, they're not keeping anyone out. They're locking us in. Locking us into forgetting that immigrants built this country, for immigrants." He looked out over the crowd, his gaze resting on the faces of day laborers, teachers, and nurses like Celine. "The American Dream wasn't meant to be a toll road."

The applause began quietly and then turned into a loud ovation. An older man wearing a veterans' cap was the first to stand, followed by a young couple holding their toddler. Soon, everyone in the crowd was on their feet.

Celine watched Pedro step down from the podium, his shoulders relaxed, a mix of exhaustion and pride clear. The fight was far from over, but here, in this auditorium, with hands clasped tightly with their neighbors, it felt possible. And that was enough to keep going.

Next, Peter adjusted the microphone, his hands trembling slightly. Sweat formed on his temples, though no one could tell if it was from heat or nerves. He cleared his throat, and the conversations around him quieted.

"Two years ago," he started, voice quiet but steady, "my best friend came here on a student visa. He wanted to study engineering, to learn how to build bridges, not just between rivers but between people." A murmur of recognition spread through the crowd. "Now?" Peter's jaw clenched. "Now they're trying to deport him back to Laos."

A collective inhale. Someone in the front row muttered, "Not again."

Peter gripped the podium. "He did everything right. He enrolled in school, paid his taxes, and never even got a parking ticket. Then one day, ICE showed up at his door saying his paperwork was 'under review.'" He made air quotes; his voice layered with bitterness. "That was six months ago. Now he sits in detention, waiting to be deported from the only home he's known for nearly a decade."

The crowd shifted uncomfortably. An elderly Black woman in the front row shook her head, her lips pressed into a thin line. Nearby, a young Latina organizer furiously scribbled notes, her pen stabbing into the paper.

Peter's voice rose, sharpening with anger. "This isn't new. This country has always treated Asian immigrants like we're disposable. The Chinese Exclusion Act. Japanese internment. Southeast Asian refugees hunted down for old criminal records from wars America dragged them into!"

His open fist pounded the podium, making the microphone screech. A baby in a stroller startled at the noise, and its mother shushed it absently, her eyes fixed on Peter.

He took a deep breath, forcing his hands to unclench. "They tell us to be the 'model minority,' keep your head down, don't complain. But what good did that do for my friend? What good did it do the Filipino veterans who fought for this country, then had their benefits stolen?"

The questions lingered in the air, thick as humidity. A Laotian grandmother near the stage wiped her eyes with the hem of her sleeve. A white teenager in a Sanctuary City T-shirt looked at the ground, fists shoved into his pockets.

Peter leaned into the mic one last time. "Today, we pay tribute to the Rev. Dr. Martin Luther King, Jr. and everything he stood for. This is a day when people celebrate freedom. But freedom can't just be for some of us. Not if we want it to mean anything at all."

A moment of silence. Then, claps started slowly, growing louder like thunder. Peter stepped back, his chest heaving. At least the truth was spoken. That had to count for something.

Philippe adjusted the microphone. "Look around you," he began, his deep voice filling every corner of the room. "Today, we celebrate freedom, but we also remember that freedom was never simply given. It was fought for." He paused before reaching into his bag and pulling out a small replica of the Statue of Liberty. He held it high, the green-tinted copper catching the light.

"This," he said, turning it so the crowd could see, "was a gift from the people of France in 1886, a symbol of liberty, revolution, and breaking chains." His fingers traced the statue's base deliberately, pausing at the broken shackles lying at her feet. "See these chains? They're easy to miss if you only ever see her from afar. But they're there, crushed beneath her, a reminder that she is meant to stand for liberation. For the end of bondage."

A murmur spread through the crowd. An older Haitian man near the front nodded solemnly and crossed his arms. A young woman in a Black Lives Matter shirt leaned forward, listening closely.

"But tell me," Philippe continued, his voice sharpening, "how can a nation display a monument to freedom with broken chains at its feet, then turn around and put new chains on people?" He swept his arm toward the crowd. "On the descendants of those who survived the Middle Passage? On those crossing deserts and oceans right now, chasing the same promise this statue claims to represent?" He looked over the gathered group. "The Statue of Liberty says, 'Give me your tired, your poor,'" Philippe recited, his tone turning bitter. "But the same country that raised her also built cages at the border. It patrols the same waters where slave ships once sailed, now hunting migrants instead." He shook his head. "We can't celebrate freedom without asking: Whose freedom still has a price? Whose chains are still waiting to be broken?"

For a moment, silence filled the room, no music, no chatter. Then, from the back, someone began to clap. Gradually, the sound grew as others joined in, until the applause swelled like waves crashing on a shore.

Philippe stepped back, wiping sweat from his brow. He understood that the real work wasn't in speeches, it was in what happened afterward.

The golden afternoon light filtered through the windows as Rosita Hernandez adjusted the microphone on the makeshift stage. "Familia," Rosita started, her voice warm but full of authority, "we stand on sacred ground today, not just because we're in this beautiful auditorium, but because Chicago has been fighting for people like us for nearly forty years."

A hush fell over the crowd as she reached into her bag and pulled out a worn photocopy. "This," she said, holding it up, "is a copy of the 1985 Sanctuary City Resolution signed by Mayor Harold Washington." The paper caught the breeze, fluttering like the flags of dozens of nations displayed around the room. "Back then, our churches were hiding Salvadoran refugees from death squads, just like some of you might be hiding neighbors from ICE today."

Near the stage, an elderly woman in a traditional dress nodded eagerly, whispering to her granddaughter. Rosita smiled at them before continuing. "And we didn't stop there. In 2006, Mayor Daley said no city employee could ask about your papers." She counted on her fingers. "2012: The Welcoming City Ordinance. 2016: We closed the loopholes ICE tried to use."

The crowd erupted into cheers, but Rosita raised a hand. "Now listen closely; this matters for all of us." She pointed at a young Black man in a 'Black Lives Matter' shirt. "Our police can't work with ICE unless there's a warrant." Then, to a group of nursing students in scrubs: "Your hospital won't report patients." Finally, to a Syrian family in the front row: "Our schools will protect your children."

Rosita's voice became urgent. "But sanctuary isn't just what the city does; it's what we do. When ICE came for our Mexican neighbors in Little Village last month, who showed up at 5 a.m., with cameras? We did."

Members in the crowd shook their heads in agreement. "So yes, Chicago is a sanctuary city since 1985," she said, wiping sweat from her brow. "But true sanctuary?" She pointed to the crowd. "That's you. That's us watching each other's backs. That's why we're here today, to celebrate how far we've come, and to fight for how much further we'll go together."

The gymnasium hummed with energy. Anyone seeking an honest word was welcomed: grandmothers in bright headwraps holding onto teenage grandsons by the wrist, weary-eyed organizers carefully arranging name tags as if laying out sacred objects. The posters along the walls displayed Dr. King's face, yes, but also lesser-known figures: Ella Baker's steady gaze, Fannie Lou Hamer's defiant smile. This was not a memorial. This was a revival.

In the cafeteria, the son of a former Freedom Rider, now a rheumatologist, led a workshop on "The Arthritis of Oppression," discussing how decades of marching, cramped jail cells, and factory shifts had hardened in Black bodies. He demonstrated stretches to loosen the shoulders of men who still recoiled at the sound of sirens. Nearby, a midwife taught mothers to check their children's cortisol levels by feeling the tightness between their shoulder blades.

A survivor of the 16th Street Baptist Church bombing sat at a folding table, tracing scars beneath her collar for a group of wide-eyed students. "They told us forgiveness was the goal," she said, showing photos of her torn choir robe. "But nobody told us how to live with the ringing in our ears afterward."

Upstairs, a therapist, herself the daughter of sharecroppers, drew a flowchart on butcher paper: "From Lynch Mobs to Microaggressions: The Same Wound, Different Bandages." Participants whispered responses like a chant: "My boss calling me 'articulate,' the cop who followed me in the grocery store, the way my son's school suspends Black boys for shouting but ignores White boys engaged in 'exuberance.'"

In the hallway, a Vietnam veteran and a Ferguson protester compared notes on tear gas. The veteran pressed a peppermint into the younger man's palm. "Suck this next time," he muttered. "Cuts the taste of riot foam."

As sunlight filtered through the high windows, a Gullah elder from the Sea Islands placed a bowl of saltwater on the stage. "Grief needs to swim," she declared, inviting attendees to stir the water with sprigs of rosemary while whispering names: Trayvon. Sandra. Freddie. Or the Haitian grandfather who was deported to a house flattened by the earthquake. The bowl became a murmuring ocean.

Dinner was served on paper plates, not charity, but communion: collards simmered with smoked turkey, cornbread dense as hope, sweet tea so sugary it made your teeth ache. The rule was simple: "No one ate alone." Lawyers balanced plates on their knees beside homeless teens. An undocumented mother spooned mashed potatoes into her toddler's mouth while a union steward distributed labor rights pamphlets in Spanglish.

Their shared meals became acts of resistance. As the last trays were cleared, a woman who'd spent the day silent suddenly stood. She was Haitian, her English halting, but she sang "Lift Every Voice" in Creole, and the room swelled with her, imperfect, overlapping, alive.

The organizers hadn't planned a finale. They didn't need to. The teach-in hadn't just shared knowledge; it had uncovered a stubborn, breathing truth: The fight was not a single event. It was a relay. And the baton was still being passed.

19

To Be or Not To Be

MARCH 2025

Celine sat at the kitchen table, her fingers tracing the rim of her untouched tea. The steam had long faded, and the honey had settled at the bottom of the cup like unresolved thoughts. The evening light filtered through the curtains, casting long shadows across the small Chicago apartment.

Philippe eased into the chair across from her as she pushed an envelope toward him. He had that look, the kind where his eyes crinkle at the corners, where his smile tries to stay small and calm but ultimately loses the battle.

He gazed at her tenderly. "They confirmed it?" he asked softly.

Celine didn't need to open the envelope to know what was inside. She had counted the days and noticed the subtle changes in her body, exhaustion, and morning queasiness. Still, seeing the test results made it all real. A life growing inside her. A child.

Her breath hitched, and for a moment, she just sat there, feeling the weight pressing on her ribs.

Philippe reached across the table, his fingers softly gripping her hand. "This is good," he whispered, examining her face. "Isn't it?"

Celine swallowed hard. Outside, tires hissed on wet pavement. News reports drifted through the thin walls, some about another immigration debate, another politician calling for harsher laws, another story about families torn apart at borders.

"Yes," she whispered. "And no."

Philippe frowned as he waited.

She turned her hand over, holding onto his. "I'm just afraid." The words came rough, edged with something deeper than fear, something closer to grief. "Afraid of bringing a child into a world where people like us are hated before we even open our mouths."

Philippe exhaled slowly, his thumb gently stroking her hand. She knew he understood. They had both heard the slurs, seen the sneers when they spoke with their subtle accents, and noticed how store clerks watched them a second too long.

Philippe leaned forward. "I know," he said. "I know it feels like the world is burning. But if we wait for it to be perfect, if we wait for people to stop hating, we'll wait forever." His voice was steady, the way it always was when he dug down to the bedrock of an issue.

Celine closed her eyes. She pictured words from the Bible, children being a heritage, a gift. Then she thought of the headlines, the raised fists at protests, the vitriol hurled at brown-skinned mothers in grocery stores.

"And what if they hurt our baby?" she whispered.

Philippe's grip tightened. "Then we show them that love is stronger. That our child is meant for more than this world's cruelty."

A tear slid down her cheek, but Celine didn't wipe it away. The fear still lingered, coiled in her stomach alongside the new life taking hold. Yet beneath it, something else stirred, delicate but persistent.

Hope.

She lifted her head. Outside, a siren wailed in the distance. The world kept spinning, brutal and beautiful all at once.

And inside her, so did the future.

The Uber arrived just as Celine checked her phone; it was ten minutes late. The car was clean but showed signs of wear, with a subtle scent of lemon cleaner and the faint aroma of old leather. She slid into the backseat, murmuring a greeting as the driver confirmed her name.

"Yes, that's me," she said, buckling her seatbelt.

The man, Jacques, according to his profile, nodded and adjusted his rearview mirror before merging into traffic. His voice was deep and steady, but his accent evoked a wave of familiarity in her. Haitian.

Celine hesitated for a moment before settling into the warm rhythm of home. "You're from Haiti?"

His eyes flicked to hers in the mirror, surprised, then softened. "Forty-five years here, but yes. You?"

"Port-au-Prince originally. I've been here since the earthquake," she said. "But Chicago feels less like home every day."

A bitter chuckle escaped him. "Tell me about it."

Rain fogged the windshield, turning streetlights into streaks. Celine watched the city blur by with people hustling under umbrellas, police lights flashing in the distance. "You ever think about going back?"

Jacques was silent for a long moment. Then, with a slow exhale: "Every day nowadays," he explained. "I have land," he said finally. "In the countryside, near Jacmel. No gangs there, not like the city. And with what I've saved, I could live like a king." His voice was wistful, but something uneasy lingered beneath it.

Celine sensed the hesitation. "But?"

He shook his head. "But will it still feel like mine after all this time? America was supposed to be different." His grip tightened on the wheel. "You hear them talk, saying 'all men created equal,' 'God bless America, ' but where's the love? The mercy? Back home, you're a child of God or you're not. No hiding. Here?" He bared his teeth in something too sharp to be a smile. "Fakes. The whole country is built on faking."

A news bulletin crackled over the radio, another story about border policies tightening like a noose. Jacques brushed it off aggressively.

Celine's chest hurt. She thought of Philippe, of the baby growing inside her, and of the world waiting to tell that child who they could be.

"You think you'll leave soon?" she asked softly.

Jacques sighed, shoulders slumping. "I still haven't decided." He laughed, but it was a hollow sound. "Funny thing, I ran from hardship, only to find a different kind here. At least in Haiti, the struggle is honest."

The car slowed as they approached the medical center, bright banners fluttering in the damp wind. Celine hesitated before stepping out. "I hope you find peace," she said. "Wherever home is."

Jacques met her eyes in the mirror. For a moment, they just looked at each other, two strangers connected by a land that the world both misunderstood and despised.

"Take care of yourself, sister," he murmured.

Then the door shut, and the car drove off, leaving her standing in the rain.

Outside, the Chicago wind rattled the windowpanes, and a chill seeped into their apartment. Philippe leaned against the counter beside Celine. Her eyes were fixed on the Form N-400. He watched her for a long moment, his eyes tracing the tension in her shoulders before he spoke.

"You've been quiet all evening," he said. "Something's on your mind."

Celine exhaled, her breathing slowing. "I've been thinking about naturalization."

Philippe raised an eyebrow. "Thinking, or rethinking?"

She turned to face him, her dark eyes flickering with doubt. "What if this isn't the right path? Am I ready to stand before a judge and swear allegiance to a flag, to a country that still treats people like bargaining chips?"

Philippe took a slow sip of coffee, letting the bitterness sit on his tongue. "You're not wrong to question it," he said. "But citizenship means protection. Stability. For us, and for the baby."

Celine rubbed her temple. "I know. But at what cost? Pledging loyalty to a democracy that's failing its people?" She pointed toward the faded spines of history books on their small living room shelf. "How many expats have left for good? Many of them left for personal reasons. Writers, artists, activists, people who once believed in the promise, just like I did."

She didn't recall them all, but some names still lingered: James Baldwin's disillusioned exile in France, Nina Simone's bitter departure to Liberia. Many believed America's ideals were just polished lies.

Philippe set his mug down, and his voice softened. "You're afraid that citizenship will make you complicit."

A sharp breath escaped her. "Yes. What if I raise my hand and swear it, only to wake up one day feeling like I've betrayed everything I believe?"

The hum of the refrigerator filled the silence. Philippe reached out, his fingers brushing hers. "Or, what if staying gives you the power to hold this country accountable?" he said carefully.

Celine hesitated.

He squeezed her hand. "Democracy doesn't die when people stop believing in it. It dies when they stop demanding better."

A distant siren wailed outside, fading as it rushed past. Celine closed her eyes, imagining their child; would they grow up resenting her for leaving, or thanking her for staying and fighting? "It feels like my demands these days are going unheard. I just need some time," she murmured.

Philippe nodded and pressed a kiss to her forehead. "Then take it. But remember that promises aren't just things governments make. They're things we keep. We the people."

Outside, the wind howled, but the kitchen remained warm, holding them in its fragile light just a little longer.

The Chicago skyline blurred into a watercolor of gray and amber streetlights as spring rain tapped against the window. Philippe leaned against the kitchen counter, stirring honey into his tea with the careful precision of someone used to accuracy. The scent of chamomile floated through the air, gentle amid the storm's staccato.

Celine sat at the kitchen table, her fingers tracing restless circles on the spine of a borrowed library book on governance and power. "What really makes democracy different?" she asked, voice low. "Not just in theory, but in the bones of everyday life?"

Philippe exhaled through his nose, as he always did before diving into complex questions, and gently set his mug down with a soft clink. "It's about where the fear lives," he said.

Celine raised an eyebrow. "Fear?"

"There are many different forms of government, Celine. Only a few of them place power in the hands of the people."

Celine breathed deeply in frustration. But she trusted Philippe's journalistic knowledge and continued to listen intently.

"In autocracy, for example," Philippe said, tucking his hands into the pockets of his worn sweater, "the people are afraid of the government. Journalists disappear. Protesters vanish. You learn to measure your words like they were rationed." He paused, his gaze drifting to the window where rain streaked the glass like fingerprints. "In democracy, real democracy, the government should be afraid of the people. Or at least accountable to them."

Celine leaned forward. "But is it?"

Philippe gave a humorless chuckle. "Depends on the day. The moment leaders stop growing indignant at public outrage, the moment courts no longer check their power, that's when democracy starts hollowing out. In my opinion, democracy is not perfect, but it is preferable to the alternatives. We, the people, have the power to stand as witnesses to its flaws. Then, through our votes, we have the power to mend the cracks in its foundation."

Celine tapped the cover of the book. "So voting is just the starting point."

"It's the bare minimum." Philippe pushed off the counter and sat across from her, elbows on his knees. "Democracy isn't a spectator sport. It needs whistleblowers, gadflies, ordinary people willing to stand in city council meetings and say no." His voice tightened. "Autocracies don't have that. Just a single, rigid story, repeated until dissent becomes unthinkable."

Outside, a gust of wind sent the rain crashing sideways, hitting the glass loudly.

Celine bit her lip. "And yet, so many democracies slide backward. Why?"

Philippe met her eyes. He assumed his professorial mode: "Democracy can slide backward because of a mix of political, economic, and social pressures. Sometimes, autocratic leaders manipulate democratic systems to weaken checks on power. For example, in Hungary, judicial independence was dismantled, the media were silenced, and elections were rigged through gerrymandering. Democracy suffers when key institutions are undermined, such as packing courts with loyalists, silencing critics through state takeovers, or turning legislators into rubber stamps. Extreme partisanship can also destroy a democracy, especially when parties see opponents as existential threats, leading to increased political violence and threats against election officials. Misinformation harms democracy, such as false claims about election fraud or foreign interference. Another threat is wealth concentration, which often results in power concentration, happening when elites buy politicians, or through Super PACs and corporate lobbying. Finally, military and police coups, voter suppression, election fraud, and fears of foreign interference all threaten democratic processes. But here's the thing. Even flawed and messy, democracy leaves the door cracked. People can still push it open wider. Autocracy bolts it shut."

The refrigerator hummed softly in the quiet, and the television in the living room murmured the evening news.

Celine squeezed Philippe's elbow, then stood and walked to the window, watching the rain blur the city lights into streaks of gold. "So, we keep pushing," she said quietly.

Philippe joined her, shoulder brushing hers. "We keep pushing," he echoed.

Beyond the glass, the storm shifted east, leaving behind the flicker of struggling stars and the relentless pulse of a nation still finding itself.

The news played softly in the background. There was another report on Haiti's spiraling crisis, another debate about America's political future. She swiveled in her chair, frowning.

"Uncle Pierre," she began, "how did Haiti's democracy fail so completely? And could the same thing happen here?"

Pierre leaned back in his worn armchair, fingers steepled. "Ah, good question, but the two situations are not the same. But they are not so different, either." He sighed. "Haiti's democracy was strangled from birth. After independence, the world punished us for daring to be free. France demanded ransom, America invaded, and our own leaders became dictators. The institutions never had a chance."

Celine nodded. "So, it was corruption? Weak government?"

"Yes, but more than that," Pierre said. "When the people lose faith in elections, when gangs replace the police, when the courts answer to the powerful, democracy becomes a ghost. Haiti reached that point long ago."

She glanced at the TV, where pundits continued to argue over the 2024 U.S. election. "But America is stronger. It has checks and balances."

Pierre chuckled darkly. "Strength can rot from within. Remember January 6th? A mob stormed the Capitol. Politicians refused to accept defeat. That is how it starts." He tapped the newspaper on the table. "Now, elections are doubted before they even happen. Politicians call each other traitors. The courts and the laws only work if people believe in them."

"So, America is what?"

"Not Haiti," he interrupted. "Not yet. But democracy is not a machine; it is a promise. If enough people break that promise, if violence replaces voting, if truth becomes whatever the powerful say it is, then even America can fall."

A silence settled between them, heavy with unspoken fears. Outside, the first drops of rain began to fall.

###

The community center hummed with a gentle buzz of Saturday afternoon activity: kids laughing in the rec room, the consistent squeak of sneakers on the gym floor, and the occasional beep of a microwave in the small kitchenette. Celine sat across from Francine at a chipped laminate table; the sharp aroma of peppermint tea cut through the lingering smell of bleach and pine cleaner.

Francine, broad-shouldered with her locs pulled back into a thick ponytail, leaned forward, resting her elbows on the table. "You look like you're carrying the world today," she observed, stirring honey into her tea. "What's on your mind?"

Celine wrapped her hands around the mug, letting the warmth seep into her palms. "I've been thinking about contradictions," she said. "How this country claims to be built on equality and democracy, but the two keep tripping over each other."

Francine smirked. "Ah. The great American tightrope walk."

"Exactly," Celine exhaled. "Take welfare programs. They are good in theory. Lift people. But then you hear folks say it makes people lazy, that it traps them. So, do we scrap them and call that freedom? Or keep them and risk creating dependency?"

Francine tapped her spoon against the rim of her mug. "And who gets to decide? That's the democracy piece. Majority votes, but what if the majority doesn't care about the folks at the bottom?"

Outside, a group of teenagers passed by the window, their voices loud and overlapping. One of them threw a basketball in the air, catching it with a smack.

Celine watched them, her brow furrowed. "It's like we're all shouting about fairness, but nobody agrees on what fair means. You want to tax the rich? Some call that justice; others call it theft. You let the market run free? Equality takes a backseat to whoever runs the fastest."

Francine nodded slowly. "And the minute you try to fix it, you hit bureaucracy. Layers and layers of it, like trying to run in wet sand." She shook her head. "I see it every day here. Want to start a job-training program? Fill out twenty forms, wait six months, and by then, half the folks who needed it will have moved on."

A toddler squealed in the play corner, and Francine's gaze flickered toward the sound, instinctive and gentle.

Celine followed her gaze. "Then there's the kids," she murmured. "Mine's going to grow up in this mess. Do I teach them to fight the system or work around it? Do I teach them to give up and give in or stand their ground?"

Francine turned back, her expression softening. "Good questions. Democracy's a tool, not a guarantee. And equality?" She shrugged. "It's not a finish line. It's the march."

The basketball outside thudded against the pavement, steady as a heartbeat.

Celine took a sip of tea, the mint sharp on her tongue. "So, we just live in the tension?"

Francine chuckled softly and warmly. "Honey, tension's where the work gets done." She reached across the table, squeezing Celine's wrist. "You don't have to solve it today. Just don't stop asking the questions."

The microwave beeped again, faint but persistent. Somewhere, a child yelled, "My turn!"

Celine smiled, small but confident. "Guess that's democracy in action."

Francine raised her mug in a half-toast. "Messy as it is." They clinked cups, the sound ringing clear above the noise.

20

A Call to Action

A few days later, at the long conference table in the church library, Celine sat across from Bradley, who was a retired social studies teacher with a rag-tag beard and a constant look of patient curiosity. His "Democracy in Action" button was slightly crooked on his sweater vest.

Celine tapped her pen against her notebook. "I keep hearing people say democracy is dying. But what is it, really? Just voting every few years?"

Bradley chuckled, adjusting his wire-rimmed glasses. "Ah, the million-dollar question." He slid a dog-eared pocket Constitution across the table toward her. "At its core? It's the idea that power belongs to the people, not kings, not oligarchs. The catch is that the people have to use it."

Celine frowned. "But if it's about the consent of the governed, why does half the country feel like they're being governed without consent?"

Bradley leaned forward, elbows on his knees. "Because democracy isn't a machine, it's a garden. It needs constant tending. Free elections?" He counted on his fingers. "Meaningful only if voters have real choices. Rule of law? Only if it applies equally to the rich and the poor." His voice dropped. "And rights? They're just words unless people fight to keep them."

A moth flew into the window screen, drawn to the light.

Celine watched it struggle. "So, when corporations buy politicians or states gerrymander districts, is that the garden withering?"

"Exactly," Bradley sighed. "The founders feared factions. Jefferson called democracy messy. But the alternative?" He gestured toward a poster on the wall, a black-and-white photo of a suffrage march. "Autocracy doesn't give you protest signs. Or the right to do this." He pointed at the poster.

The coffee maker gurgled in the corner, its bitter aroma mixing with the scent of rain through the propped-open door.

Celine bit her lip. "Then why does participation feel like shouting into the wind?"

"Because democracy's slow," Bradley softened. "But remember, women couldn't vote. Poll taxes existed. Remember when Black people counted as three-fifths of a person? Change happens when people refuse to quit." He pushed a voter guide toward her. "You're part of the 'we' in 'We the People.' Even when it's hard."

A basketball hit the building's siding, followed by giggles and scattered apologies.

Celine smiled softly and picked up the guide. "So, tending the garden just means showing up?"

Bradley stood, stretching his back. "And pulling weeds. And planting new seeds." He nodded at the teens outside. "And sometimes, making sure the next generation knows how to dig."

She slipped the booklet into her bag as the first raindrops tapped against the pavement, soft, insistent, alive.

###

That afternoon, Celine sat across from Pastor Eli at a folding table, her fingers tracing the figure of an angel on this week's church bulletin. The pastor, lean and steady with salt-and-pepper stubble, leaned back in his chair. His sleeves were rolled up, revealing forearms that still carried the wiry strength of a man who had grown up hauling feed bags on his grandfather's farm. His eyes, however, remained gentle, always listening.

"You've been carrying something heavy," he observed. "What's weighing on you?"

Celine exhaled. "Equality," she said. "I've been grappling with the idea of a truly equal society." She hesitated. "What does the Kingdom of God say about it?"

Pastor Eli smiled, the creases around his eyes deepening. "Ah. 'The first will be last, and the last will be first.'" He took a slow sip of coffee. "You're asking if God wants us to live in a world where no one gets left behind."

"Yes," Celine said. "But here's the tension: man says, 'equal opportunity,' but then resists sharing resources. Man says 'justice,' but balks at redistribution. How do we live equality when everything in this world fights against it?"

Outside, the church van roared to life; a youth group member laughed, their voice blending with the distant rumble of traffic.

The pastor set his cup down carefully. "Remember the feeding of the five thousand? Jesus didn't ask who'd brought bread and who hadn't. He didn't ask where the followers were from or demand they prove their worth. He took what was offered, blessed it, and made sure everyone ate." His fingers tapped the laminate table. "That's the Kingdom. Not just equal chance, but equal provision."

Celine frowned. "But we're not first-century peasants sharing fish. We're in a system where some hoard billions while others ration insulin."

"True." Pastor Eli's gaze sharpened. "So, the question is, how can we be like the boy who offered his loaves? How do we challenge the systems of oppression while still feeding the hungry right now?"

She rubbed her temples. "It's just frustrating. You say, 'do justice,' but people act like fairness is a crime."

The pastor chuckled dryly. "Funny. People often forget that Acts describes believers selling land so no one would be needy." He shook his head. "We're all created equal in God's eyes. But democracy? It's built on human nature, and human nature's corrupted by pride, fear, the instinct to hoard power."

A silence settled between them, broken only by the hum of the air conditioner.

Celine exhaled slowly. She'd turned these questions over in her mind for months, like river stones worn smooth by a constant flow. Did any of it matter? Would the world always twist justice into something conditional?

"So where does that leave us?" she finally asked.

"Working, wrestling, and trusting," Pastor Eli said, pushing back his chair. "The Kingdom's already here, just not yet finished." He nodded toward the stairs, where sunlight pooled at the threshold. "Best we get to building."

For the first time that afternoon, Celine smiled. She took a breath and followed him upstairs into the light, where the work, imperfect and urgent, awaited.

###

The next evening, the air carried the scent of damp earth as Celine sat on the back porch, her bare feet resting on the wooden slats, a half-finished sketch of a playground in her lap; it depicted swings without chains and slides without steps.

Philippe stepped outside and sat down beside her, balancing two glasses of lemonade. The condensation dripped onto his fingers as he handed her one. "You've been quiet tonight," he said.

She grasped the glass, the cold seeping into her palms. "I keep thinking about the world our kid will inherit," she admitted. "Not this one. Something different."

He leaned against the railing, the city's glow casting gold and shadow across the lines of his face. "Different how?"

"Where democracy isn't just about pulling a lever every four years," she said, "but about truly having a say in your life. Where equality isn't a buzzword but the foundation." She tapped her pencil against her sketch. "Imagine schools where funding doesn't depend on zip codes. Hospitals where care isn't a privilege. A politics that doesn't just let you participate but expects you to."

Philippe swirled the ice in his glass. "You're describing a world that doesn't exist."

"I know," she said softly. "But should that stop us from building it?"

He watched her for a long moment. "No. But it means recognizing the cracks in the foundation." His voice took on the rhythm of an old argument, one worn smooth by repetition. "Democracy's messy. People vote against their own interests. They cling to hierarchies. They say they believe in equal treatment under the law. At the same time, they fear equity because they think it means losing something instead of gaining everything."

Celine's pencil moved almost automatically, shading the edges of her sketch. "Then we change the story. We make it about common ground, not zero-sum games." She looked up. "You've seen real revolutions. You know, people can demand better."

Philippe exhaled sharply. "And then the backlash comes. The push to 'restore order,' which usually means restoring the old imbalances." He reached out, brushing a smudge of graphite off her wrist. "I'm not saying it's impossible. I'm saying it's a fight. Every day."

A breeze fluttered the edges of her paper, carrying a hint of turbulence from the west.

Celine set her sketch aside. "Then we fight," she said. "Not just for the big upheavals but the small things too: community land trusts, co-op businesses, teaching kids that fairness isn't a fantasy." She met his gaze. "I won't raise my child to lower their expectations."

Philippe's thumb brushed along the rim of his glass. "You'll exhaust yourself."

"Maybe." She smiled faintly. "But I'd rather burn out than rust."

For a while, they sat quietly, listening to the city breathe, the distant laughter from a nearby balcony, the rhythmic clatter of a train crossing the bridge.

Finally, Philippe reached for her sketch and tilted it toward the light. "No chains on the swings, huh?"

"None," she said. "If we start with the playgrounds, who knows where we might end up?"

He kissed her temple, his lips warm on her skin. "Alright, dreamer," he murmured. "Let's get to work."

Above them, the first star of the evening flickered to life, a tiny point of light in the growing dark.

Outside Celine's apartment, the wind howled, rattling the windowpanes and stirring the fine layer of dust that had seeped in through unseen cracks. Celine lounged on the sofa to watch the evening news. Most days, the stories were disturbing and made her sad. Today, a news reporter warned that the same chaos that plagued Los Angeles could occur in Chicago if the President carried out his threat to send troops to conduct ICE raids in Chicago.

The television flickered with chaotic images as Celine fixed her gaze on the televised scene: riot gear, tear gas, bodies pressed against each other beneath a veil of swirling dust. The wind howled like a living creature, tearing at protest signs and sending fast-food wrappers and newspaper scraps spiraling into the turbulent air. The thick smoke of tear gas mixed with the thin cloud of sandy dust, making the crowds blink and cough as they surged forward, then pulled back.

Bodies pressed together, a mosaic of rage and desperation, college students in gas masks, grandmothers linking arms, construction workers with bandanas tied over their mouths. Their voices rose in a furious chorus against the rhythmic thud of batons on riot shields. "Stop the deportations!" A water bottle flew through the air, exploding against the side of an armored National Guard vehicle.

Then, the first pops of rubber bullets.

A young woman in a yellow hoodie screamed as someone grabbed her thigh, causing her to collapse onto the asphalt. Strangers pulled her back, her sneakers leaving bloodied trails on the pavement. The line of soldiers advanced, faceless behind visors, their rifles raised.

Outside his church, a priest stood with his arms outstretched, his vestments flapping wildly in the grit-filled wind. "This is a house of worship!" he shouted at the approaching troops, pointing to the church behind him, its doors wide open, with people huddled inside. A soldier pushed past him.

At the intersection, flames consumed a police cruiser. The intense heat warped the air, casting eerie shadows on the faces of the protesters surrounding it, their hands raised and their voices raw, while the world was transformed into a feverish dream of silhouettes and sirens.

The news anchor's voice was calm and clinical, as if describing a disaster movie instead of real events. Federal troops mobilized. Rubber bullets deployed. Three confirmed dead, seventeen injured. Undocumented families, asylum seekers, and even legal residents were swept up indiscriminately.

Celine's cell phone rang. It was Francine. "They're gathering in the Lincoln Park neighborhood," she said frantically. "ICE agents are rounding up people at Wrightwood Park. We need observers. Can you come help out? Now?"

Celine grabbed her jacket, hesitated for a moment, then pulled it on. The screen still blared behind her as she left, the riot swelling, the storm rolling in.

The wind swept through Wrightwood Park, lifting dust and creating a haze over the crowd at the annual Taco and Tequila Fest. Celine adjusted her neon green hat embossed with "Observer." She tightened her grip on her cell phone and began recording the scene on video.

All around her, the plaza buzzed with tension, a volatile mix of celebration and anger. To her left, revelers gathered under colorful banners, the air alive with the sound of mariachi music. Restaurant vendors displayed their food in tents. People from different ethnic backgrounds moved through the crowd. Parents held their children's hands tightly; their laughter tinged with fragile caution.

"They're afraid," Celine observed aloud. "But they came anyway."

To her right, away from the festivities, the anti-ICE protesters stood in solidarity. Faith leaders in clerical collars prayed aloud, their voices steady despite the nervous chatter. A Latina woman with a megaphone called out the names of deportees, each syllable sharp and clear. Nearby, a Black reverend linked arms with a White rabbi, their presence a silent protest against the masked ICE agents lurking at the edges. "No human is illegal!" shouted a group of college students, their signs shaking in the wind.

And then, ICE.

They moved like shadows in tactical gear, faces concealed by black masks and mirrored sunglasses. Their presence was a silent threat, a tightly coiled viper ready to strike. Celine's pulse quickened as she observed their movements, noting how they hovered around the edges of the crowd, their hands near zip-ties and batons. One agent stared directly at a teenage boy in a "Viva Mexico" shirt, nostrils flaring as if scenting prey.

The air pulsed like a battlefield.

Then, chaos.

A bottle burst like a gunshot against the pavement, with glass shards skittering across the concrete and glinting in the midday sun. A startled gasp rippled through the crowd just before the scream, piercing and raw as it cut through the rising noise. Near the metal barricades, an ICE agent in a navy-blue vest yanked a young man forward by the arm, his sneakers slipping on the asphalt as he struggled to keep his footing.

"Stop! He's a citizen!" The voice belonged to a gray-haired woman leaning over the barrier, her knuckles white where she gripped it. No one listened.

More agents moved in, their commands sharp, robotic, drilled into them through procedure and policy. "Turn around! Hands behind your back!" But the young man was already on his knees, fingers laced behind his head, his breath coming in ragged bursts. The crowd seethed. Some backed away, others surged forward. Protesters locked arms, forming a human chain that swayed against the crush of bodies.

The Reverend's voice cut above it all, deep and resonant from the makeshift stage. "We will not be divided by fear!" But fear was already there, choking the air, thick as the dust swirling up from a nearby construction pit.

Celine's fingers gripped the camera as she recorded every movement. Captured every expression. The sunlight highlighted the tear tracks on the woman's cheeks beside her, her sobs muffled behind trembling hands. A child, no older than six, clung to his mother's leg and yelled, not in protest, but in pure fear.

Closest to the van, a scuffle erupted. A young protester in a denim jacket lunged, only to be grabbed by two agents and pushed backward. The van doors slammed shut, locking whoever was inside. The engine roared to life.

And through it all, Celine watched. Wide-eyed. Burning every detail into memory.

The dust settled slowly. The crowd heaved like a wounded animal. Somewhere, a lone voice started chanting. Others joined in, initially weak, then stronger. The Reverend raised a fist. The agents moved back into formation. The protest wasn't over. But something had already been broken. A line had already been drawn.

In defiance, Celine stood her ground, kept her camera steady, and let it witness the pain, the defiance, the break, and the confusion. She did not flinch. She did not falter. She did not look away. She continued recording until her camera's battery died.

21

New Life Coming

The late autumn wind clawed at the windows of their second-floor apartment, rattling the panes in their loose frames. A brittle draft seeped through the old wood, carrying the scent of damp leaves and the distant hum of evening traffic. The radiator hissed in uneven bursts, fighting a losing battle against the creeping Chicago chill.

Celine sat hunched over the kitchen table, the Form N-400 spread before her like an unread prophecy. Her hands, still dotted with tiny scars from years of hospital sanitizer, cradled a chipped mug of lemon tea from her aunt's summer garden. The steam had long since disappeared, leaving behind the ghost of citrus and earth. She traced the rim absentmindedly, her fingernail catching on a hairline crack.

Across from her, Philippe watched with the patient stillness of a man who knows when to wait. The dim kitchen light caught the silver in his temples, and the shadows deepened the lines between his brows. His own tea sat untouched, a lukewarm puddle gathering at the bottom of the cup.

"You've been staring at those papers for twenty minutes," he finally said. His voice was gentle, but in the quiet apartment, it could have been a shout. "You qualify in every way. What's holding you back?"

Celine exhaled sharply through her nose, a sound full of unspoken arguments. Outside, a loose shutter slammed against the brick in an erratic rhythm. "Sounds like gunshots in Port-au-Prince," she thought, then quickly pushed the memory away.

"It's not about qualifications," she said. She could feel the words thickening in her throat, clogging like the phlegmy coughs of the COVID patients she'd intubated in the spring of 2020. Back when the world had narrowed to the smell of bleach and the way her N95 straps carved grooves into her cheeks.

Philippe said nothing. He had learned in their years of shared life that silence was more effective than prodding or logic. The truth flowed into empty spaces like water seeping through cracks. Like water, the truth sought its own level.

She tapped the form, the Oath of Allegiance section glaring up at her in bureaucratic bold. "I know what they want. Swear loyalty. Renounce Haiti like it's some rival lover. Recite lines about defending a Constitution that didn't defend my cousin when ICE picked him up outside the 7-Eleven last year." Her voice stayed clinically even, the way it did when she explained a terminal diagnosis to grieving families. But Philippe heard the tremor underneath, the raw nerve.

"You remember Del Rio?" The question wasn't really a question. The images haunted her some nights: Haitian men with their wrists zip-tied, women clutching toddlers while Border Patrol agents on horseback loomed like a scene from the Old West. A visceral echo of the slave patrols their ancestors had fled. "They treat us like we're not human."

"Contagious," Philippe added quietly. "They treat us like we're contagious." He had seen it too, in how patients at the clinic sometimes recoiled when they heard his accent, and in the way politicians said "Haitian gang members" as if it were a single word.

Celine's grip tightened around the mug. A memory surfaced, her first day at the hospital, the charge nurse eyeing her credentials with evident skepticism. "Your English is so good," the woman had said, as if she'd expected grunts and pidgin.

She pressed her free hand to her belly's swell, where their son wiggled restless somersaults. "And what about him?"

Philippe leaned forward. "Listen to me," he said, his thumb brushing the rigid tendon in her wrist. "That baby will never doubt his right to be here. But Celine, you earned this. You, with your nursing license, your perfect credit score, and your dedicated attendance at community welfare meetings. They don't get to make you feel like a beggar at the table."

A siren wailed down the street, its sound piercing through the apartment before fading into the city's white noise. Celine's gaze shifted to the gallery wall by the fridge, where her memories lived in frames. The largest photograph, its edges softened by time, showed her mother dancing under a lavender twilight in Haiti, feet kicking up dust, her bright dress caught mid-swirl. Celine had taken the picture years ago, long before the ground split open and stole everything. Still, she never looked at it without hearing the echo of her mother's laughter, reckless and full, as if disaster had been unthinkable.

Beside it hung a print of Celine standing stiff-shouldered in her nursing scrubs after graduation day, diploma clutched in both hands like a shield. The frame was cheap plastic, but she kept it because Philippe, still an acquaintance back then, had crept into the shot, grinning over her shoulder as if he already knew he'd stick around. Sometimes, when exhaustion made her hands tremble after a double shift, she would trace the shadow of his arm near the edge of the photo and remember how solid he'd felt the first time he steadied her.

A blur of flag-wrapped protesters, their faces hidden behind scarves, filled another frame. It was a grainy cellphone shot from a protest in Washington Park, one the news cameras ignored, but she had tucked it here because it proved she hadn't stayed silent. In the corner of the picture, the corner of her own sign jutted into view, the words now half-faded but seared into her memory: "They cannot erase us."

The newest addition was a snapshot of a windowsill crowded with meal containers, hands in latex gloves passing food to an elderly neighbor during the lockdowns. That one wasn't pretty, but it stayed because it reminded her of the desperation and stubborn kindness of those months, how they'd fed each other when the world outside was coming apart.

And then there was the space in the middle. Not vacant by accident, but waiting. Philippe had left a scrap of paper there once, scribbled with a promise in blue ink, and even though she could have moved it, she never did. Some gaps need to stay open, just a little longer, until the correct memory comes to fill them.

Her wall was covered with memories of a life constructed brick by brick in the gaps between belonging and exile.

"I don't regret coming," she whispered. The admission settled between them, fragile as the first frost on the windowpane. "But Philippe, how do I swear loyalty to a country that keeps proving it sees us as conditional citizens? Like we're only allowed to stay as long as we're useful?"

Philippe's hand closed over hers, warm and confident.

"Don't pledge to what America is," he said, his voice rough from the weight of his own father's deportee ankle monitor, his brother's TPS renewal nightmares. "Pledge to what we're forcing it to become."

The radiator sputtered, and somewhere in the walls, pipes groaned like old bones.

Celine looked down at the form. The blank line at the bottom blurred under her unshed tears, the letters swimming into gibberish. For now, the papers remained untouched.

But tomorrow. Tomorrow was another battle.

The aroma of roasted garlic and thyme filled the apartment as Celine stirred the hearty stew. Outside, the late afternoon sun hung low in the sky, its light softened by a strange, milky haze that blurred the edges of the Chicago skyline.

Philippe sat at the kitchen table, scrolling through his phone. "They're saying the air quality advisory is in effect until Friday," he muttered, frowning at the screen. "Canadian wildfires. The smoke's drifting all the way down here."

Uncle Pierre, standing by the window with a glass of red wine, squinted at the horizon. "It's not just the fires," he said, tapping the glass. "They imploded that old factory over on 12th last week. Dust's still settling. Now it's mixing with the smoke, like breathing sandpaper." He took a sip, his mustache twitching. "Used to be, you could see the Sears Tower clear as day from here."

Celine wiped her hands on her apron and joined him at the window. The air outside had an eerie, amber tint, as if the world were viewed through old glass. She could taste it, a faint grit on her tongue, a film at the back of her throat. "It's not just here," she said softly. "The whole planet's choking."

Philippe exhaled sharply. "And yet, we're still arguing about whether climate change is real."

Pierre chuckled darkly. "People will debate the color of the sky while it burns."

Celine absentmindedly rubbed her lower back, a habit she'd picked up in her third trimester. "What kind of world are we bringing this baby into?"

Philippe put his phone down. "One where we teach them to fight for better."

Pierre turned from the window, swirling his wine. "You got your nursery list ready? Can't fight anything without supplies."

Celine offered a faint smile and reached for a notepad on the counter. "Diapers, onesies, a bassinet. "

"And an air purifier," Philippe interjected. "A good one."

Pierre nodded. "Smart. And maybe some plants. Spider lilies. They scrub toxins."

Celine scribbled it down, her pencil scratching against the paper. Outside, a siren wailed in the distance, muffled by the thick air.

No one spoke for a moment. The haze pressed against the windows.

Then Philippe reached over and squeezed Celine's hand. "We'll figure it out," he said. "One breath at a time."

Pierre raised his glass. "To clean air," he said, "and the people stubborn enough to demand it."

He and Philippe clinked their drinks together as the sun sank lower into the smoke, tinting the room in shades of copper and rust.

Tools cluttered the living room floor: Allen wrenches, mismatched screws, and a hastily printed instruction manual that Philippe kept flipping upside down in frustration. The crib's wooden slats rested in a chaotic semi-circle around them like the bones of some uncooperative beast.

Celine rubbed her temples. "It says Part B connects to Slot D, but there's no Slot D."

Uncle Pierre, kneeling next to a misshapen drawer in his flannel shirt, squinted at the confusing black-and-white diagrams. "These things are designed to make men feel useless," he muttered.

The television hummed softly in the corner, with a news anchor's steady voice cutting through their struggle: "U.S. deploys National Guard to Chicago and Atlanta as protests over the new immigration bill turn violent. Meanwhile, Russian forces advance near Kharkiv."

Philippe exhaled sharply, tossing the manual aside. "Every time we try to build something, the world's busy tearing itself apart."

A shadow flickered across Celine's face as she struggled to align two panels that refused to fit together. The baby, their baby, would sleep in this crib and grow up in this world. A world where autocrats waved nuclear threats while their streets filled with soldiers in camouflage, and entire cities were erased pixel by pixel on the news scroll.

"Empires do fall," Pierre said, tapping a screwdriver against his palm. "But not fast enough."

The newscast switched to Gaza: rubble where hospitals once stood, a dust-covered child's face staring blankly at the camera.

Celine's hands paused on the wood.

Philippe noticed her expression. "Hey." He reached over and squeezed her wrist. "We're not doomed yet."

Pierre snorted. "Optimism. Cute. But history's a pendulum, swings toward tyranny, then swings back."

Outside, a car alarm sounded briefly before going silent. The instruction manual fluttered in the breeze from the open window, smelling of distant smoke.

Celine picked up a screw. "Then we build it anyway," she said quietly. "Even if the instructions are wrong."

For a while, the only sounds were the clink of metal, the shuffle of wood, and the murmurs of news, wars, warnings, and the scrape of something fragile against the teeth of the world.

Then, with a click, the first drawer smoothly slid into place.

The September air clung to them like a damp cloth as they walked toward the church, with cicadas humming in the thick oak trees lining the street. Celine carried a basket of homemade bread, her offering for the fellowship breakfast, while Philippe fidgeted with his tie knot, the morning heat already darkening his collar with sweat. Uncle Pierre, always the storyteller, adjusted his wide-brimmed hat as a local news reporter's voice crackled through the nearby car radio.

Tropical Storm Lorenzo has reached Category 1 strength and was expected to intensify as it moves through the Caribbean,

Pierre exhaled slowly and heavily. "Seems like every year now, the sea starts tossing its tantrums our way." His voice was low, carrying the weight of decades spent studying weather patterns, not just as a sailor but as a man who'd learned to see storms as both threats and testaments.

Celine watched the shifting play of sunlight on their faces, the reddish-gold of late summer caught in Philippe's frown, the bronze skepticism in Pierre's squint. "You know," she mused, adjusting the cloth napkin covering the bread, "It never stops. Not the storms, not the rebuilding. Like clockwork."

Philippe's phone buzzed with an update; he silenced it with a thumb swipe. "You'd think by now, with satellites and forecasts, we'd find some way to tame them."

Pierre chuckled, a sound like dry leaves crackling. "Tame a hurricane? Boy, we used to watch them roll in like uninvited relatives, devastating but inevitable. And yet." He gestured toward a cluster of blue morning glories climbing a neighbor's fence, their petals trembling under the weight of a bumblebee. "People still plant. They still build."

Celine reflected on the split-open roofs in Puerto Rico after Maria, and Haiti's concrete homes that stubbornly stood through flood after flood. She thought of the baby, their baby, soon to enter a world where disasters spun like tops, but communities rallied around their members.

"The ocean doesn't check with the weatherman," Philippe muttered almost to himself.

Pierre patted his shoulder. "Nor did Pharaoh consult Moses, but the Red Sea parted anyway. Earth's the Lord's, not the developer's, not the dictator's. Storms serve as a reminder."

Celine touched her belly where her life softly kicked against her ribs, and she smiled. "So, we plant anyway."

They walked toward the steeple as the bell rang ahead. And even though the news mentioned deadly winds, the cicadas continued to sing, unfazed.

The hospital room was spotless and sterile. Dull fluorescent lights buzzed overhead, their reflection shimmering on the vinyl floors. Outside the freshly polished window, dusk settled over Chicago in streaks of flame-orange and bruised violet. Simultaneously, the indifferent skyline shimmered coldly as another contraction hit Celine with the force of a tidal wave.

The fetal monitor's mechanical beep quickened as Celine arched against the thin mattress, her hospital gown sticking to her back like a second skin. Philippe's large hand fully cupped hers, his thumb nervously rubbing circles over the scars from years tending to others. In the corner, Uncle Pierre, still dressed in his deacon's suit from the evening service, paced in the waiting room like a caged lion, his polished shoes squeaking against the linoleum with each turn. Every few steps, he paused to swipe at his glistening forehead with the same embroidered handkerchief he had carried since the earthquake.

Another contraction tore through Celine, sharper this time. White sparks exploded behind her eyelids as monitors screeched in protest. Philippe's reassurances dissolved into meaningless noise as the pain made her mind reel backward, past the nurse's station's blinking monitors, past the "Welcome to Chicago" billboard she saw upon arriving in the city, all the way to the sunbaked pier in Port-de-Paix where she boarded a fishing boat for the first time.

"You always wanted more," she imagined her grandmother whispering against her hair, the words heavy with generations of similar admonitions. The memory now darkened as another monitor shrieked. More what? More fluorescent-lit suffering? More nights jumping at every siren outside their apartment, wondering if ICE vans were trolling Rogers Park again?

"Breathe, my love," Philippe urged, smoothing back her sweat-soaked braids with trembling fingers. The gold band on his left hand caught the light, bought with hard-earned wages from his job at the newspaper. He had the ring resized three times as his weight fluctuated with stress.

His touch anchored her just enough for her to notice the patronizing mural across the hallway, some corporate artist's vision of diverse babies floating in saccharine unity. One cherubic brown face grinned forever beside the fire escape, oblivious to the truth: that this hospital's board had fought against Medicaid expansion last fiscal year.

The contraction crested. Celine's vision tunneled as she gasped. The veteran nurse adjusted Celine's IV while the doctor bustled in, her purple gloves snapping against her wrists as she checked the monitor. "Nine centimeters," she announced with the hollow cheer of someone nearing the end of their shift.

Celine barely heard her. The baby's heartbeat thundered through the speakers now, a staccato drumbeat that merged with the old rhythms from her childhood. Another contraction hit like a truck.

"Push!" the doctor ordered.

Celine howled as she pushed with all her might. In the intense, white-hot pain, she suddenly realized that this suffering was the price of belonging. The monitor's shriek mingled with her scream.

Then, she heard her son's first furious cry as he entered the world, slick with defiance.

When they placed the squalling infant on her chest, Celine traced his crumpled ear, a replica of Philippe's, and laughed through her tears.

Outside, the first autumn rain began to fall. Somewhere beyond the hospital walls, politicians were still arguing about birthright citizenship in air-conditioned offices. Here in this cramped room, sticky with new life and ancient hopes, her son's fingernails scraped against her collarbone.

Later, Uncle Pierre's calloused hand caressed the infant's head. "Look at this warrior," he murmured as the infant's impossibly dark eyes met the world. Outside, the rain fell harder, each drop pounding against the window of a country that now had no choice but to reckon with him.

Off the coast of Haiti, another hurricane was forming in the Caribbean.

www.ingramcontent.com/pod-product-compliance
Lightning Source LLC
Chambersburg PA
CBHW051140020726
47501CB00005B/1597

* 9 7 9 8 3 8 5 2 6 4 4 9 0 *